Patti Larsen

Copyright © 2011 Patti Larsen

All rights reserved.

Cover art © by Stephanie Mooney. All rights reserved.

ISBN-10: 1466276525

ISBN-13: 978-1466276529

DEDICATION

Your generosity not only helped me bring this series to life, your support and faith made me believe anything is possible.

Thank you, Renee, Sarah, Kirstin, Kelly, Nishka, Caron, Cindy, Mille, Valerie, Joan, Kim K., Kimberly, Louise, Kim M, Darlene.

Also by

PATTI LARSEN

HIDE
FIGHT*
HUNT*

CAT CITY

* (TO BE RELEASED)

This book came into being with the assistance and caring of many. I couldn't do what I do without my Mom, my sisters, my loving and supportive husband and my fabulous friends, online and off. Writing is a solitary endeavor, and without them I would be a full time hermit, lost in my own worlds with the voices inside my head.

I reached out with an IndieGoGo campaign to fund this dream and so many of you answered. With love, I thank you from the bottom of my heart. I hope you enjoy what you helped create.

1

Reid wakes in darkness. But not quiet, steady darkness like he's used to, the kind that lulls him to sleep and keeps him there. This blackness is full of motion and sound. Mind fog drifts around him, keeping his thoughts from forming clearly. He has only a moment to wonder what is happening when he is spun sideways and slammed into something hard. His right shoulder protests, recognizing the pain. It was a blow like this one that woke him in the first place.

He knows he has to sit up, instincts warring with the disorientation and confusion in his mind. Flickers of memory only taunt him, offering no answers through the curtain of mist keeping him helpless. His hands and feet feel tight, almost numb. Reid shakes his head a little, cheek pressed to something harsh that scratches against his face when he moves. It smells like plastic and rusting metal. And someone else's vomit.

At least, as far as he can tell it's someone else's.

This time when the motion sends him flying, he realizes he is in a vehicle of some kind. His mind guesses a van. Even though he can't see, he can feel the space around him, hollow and empty. Reid blinks, trying to restore his vision, but his eyelashes meet fabric over and over, fluttering against the blindfold like a desperately trapped bird. Everything he does to work it loose fails, his coordination missing. The throbbing in his temples makes it impossible to focus.

A moan rises in his throat. He can't stop it. His stomach clenches against a wave of nausea, heart beat pounding one moment before skipping erratically the next. Panic joins the party, taking him and shaking him until he finds himself thrashing against his bonds in an all-out struggle for freedom. The pounding in his head gets louder and more insistent and he can't keep it in anymore.

"Hey!" His voice is raw and jagged, throat burning. He only then realizes how thirsty he is. "What the hell! Let me out!" His protests devolve into wordless yelling, as desperate as his fight against his captivity.

It's not long before only silence emerges from his tortured throat. His strength is gone in moments. The fog in his mind is lifting, but with it comes a horrible, creeping weakness. Reid collapses, gasping for air, voice completely gone. This can't be happening. Stuff like this only happens in the movies, right? Besides, he has nothing anyone would want. Orphaned, broke, barely sixteen.

His mind spikes fearfully at the thought of being in the hands of some kind of sick pervert before shying from the idea. He does his best to flex his fingers and feet while his mind battles him for control of his body, feeling the subtle tingle of blood trying to reach his extremities. He finds if he keeps his attention on the job and it alone, he can stuff down a measure of the panic and hold himself in check.

Reid swears to himself then and there, if he is under the control of a monster like that, he will fight until one of them dies.

Someone laughs. Reid freezes, a lump of ice slamming into his already queasy stomach. But the sound is muffled, coming from in front of him, as though through a wall or panel. Another voice laughs with the first. Two of them then, as far as Reid can tell. Pedophiles don't work in pairs, do they? He has no idea, but decides not just to settle his mind.

He rolls forward as the driver hits the brakes. Reid impacts the front of the compartment with his head, his neck buckling under the strain. He cries out, twisting his body forward, face tucked to his chest. His torso slides in a semi-circle as the van comes to a hard halt, shoulders absorbing the rest of the impact. A flicker of light makes it past his blindfold and he instantly strains toward it, begging for it. More voices, new ones this time. Still muffled though, and impossible to identify.

"Help me, please! Somebody!" Reid's dull and crusty shout for attention gets him nothing. No one answers him, saves him. He is on his own.

The van starts forward again, Reid at the mercy of its momentum. He is already covered in protesting bruises and is just grateful nothing feels broken. The ride is rough and at one point he is almost weightless. Reid cries out from the shock of it, just before the van slams to a halt once more. He tucks just in time so his back bears the brunt of the assault, his body curled into a tight 'C'. Weight shifts at the front of the van. Two doors slam in rapid succession. Reid takes one more panicked moment to tear at the bonds holding him. He needs to get free before they can reach him. But they are already there. The door creaks near his feet, and cool, fresh air floods the back of the van. He wishes he could welcome it as it washes over him, but he fears the end of the journey.

Until he catches a familiar scent that shifts him into happy memory. Reid isn't sure why the smell of trees and the out doors makes him feel better, but it does. Hands grab his feet and jerk him out horizontal, dumping him on the ground, while his father's face swims in his mind. He cries out, attempting to lash around with his legs and hands, hard to do with them tied so tightly.

"Quit it, you," one voice tells him, rough and old like the edge of a rusty saw.

"Aw, let him struggle," the other laughs, nasal and piercing in the quiet. "He'll be needing the fight in him."

They both laugh then. Like this whole thing is some big joke. Reid kicks out when hands settled on him again. Bright lights flash in his head as something bony and hot impacts his jaw. He drifts into the fog, wanting to fight back, but lost in the darkness. He is only aware enough of his surroundings to understand he is being carried somewhere, but has no way to stop his captors from doing with him as they wish.

His mind tells him to quit. Reid almost listens. But his heart is too strong, his instincts taking control where his thoughts fail him. The moment he is able, he begins his struggle all over again.

"Tough little bugger," the first voice says, then grunts as Reid feels his sneaker impact something soft but firm. "Ruddy bastard!"

The second voice laughs.

"That's it," the first grouses as the world tips and shifts so Reid's feet are pointed almost at the ground, his stomach aching from the disorientation of it, "you get the damned feet next time."

The hands on him vanish. For an instant he hangs suspended in time and space. Gravity reasserts and he lands hard, flat on his back, the wind in his lungs gone from the sudden stop. Hands loosen his bonds, but he is too breathless to react to the chance of sudden freedom.

"Good luck, kid," the first voice says. One of them hocks up phlegm and spits noisily. "You're going to need it."

"Luck?" The other says, footsteps and voices fading in the distance as they leave him there. "Ain't no luck going to save him now."

Their laughter leads them out.

Alone, Reid gasps in a deep breath, then another. It hurts his ribs, his lungs. He manages to roll over on his right side and regrets it. His shoulder roars in protest. Still, he is finally able to wriggle his numb hands loose from what holds him and claw at the cloth around his eyes.

Darkness. But not complete. The moon is up. Trees loom over him, the smell of spruce and fresh air so sharp it almost hurts. He doesn't take the time to look around, not yet, but jerks at the plastic ties that hold his ankles, gasping in pain as the circulation returns to his useless fingers. His vision swims through a veil of pain-laden tears, but he manages somehow to force his screaming hands to work the ties loose and he is free.

Reid's first instinct is to bolt. When he tries, he collapses immediately. His feet suffer the same fate as his hands. He spends a long time writhing on the ground in the dirt, suffering the agony of long-lost blood flow.

By the time he is able to wipe the tears from his face and sit up, the moon overhead has moved a fair distance. Reid tries to stand again and manages to get to his knees. He half walks, half crawls his way forward, his aching hands finding the bark of a thick tree. Touching it makes everything worse, because the roughness of it proves this nightmare is real.

Reid uses the support of the oak to haul himself upright. He leans back against the gnarled trunk and fights to get his bearings, physically and mentally. His tongue runs over his teeth, furry with bacteria, an odd taste in his mouth making him gag. He works up some saliva and swishes it around, spitting it out like his captor did. The act of leaning forward to do so almost puts him back on his knees as a wave of dizziness sends him reeling.

Reid clutches at the trunk again and hugs it, keeping himself upright, desperately grateful for its steadfast strength. He would have never thought before that night a lowly tree could be his best friend.

He is feeling better, more alert, but the weariness still clings to him, the haze in his head slow to lift. He wants to collapse to the ground and close his eyes, to sleep and pretend this isn't happening. But he knows that isn't an option. No more than letting some pervert have his way with him. Reid has to get out of there.

Where is there exactly? He has no way of finding out, not from where he is standing. In his struggle to be upright he got turned around and hasn't a clue which way the voices went when they left him. And why kidnap him only to dump him in the woods? None of it makes sense. But Reid doesn't care about any of that right now. All he cares about is going home.

At least there is a path. He can see it winding through the trees. Reid tries to scan further ahead and spots an upgrade. He remembers being carried like he was descending and a wave of relief, his first since this started, washes through him. His lips twist into a grin. Idiots. They totally gave it away. Now he knows where to go.

He gathers himself for another moment before trying to walk. It's surprisingly easy considering what he's gone through. His feet have recovered enough he can feel the roughness of the path through his sneakers. Reid is grateful his captors didn't do any permanent damage. A broken bone or two would have made what he is trying much harder, if not impossible. But he is in relatively good shape, a natural athlete, and figures with enough time and rest he'll find his way out.

After a few staggered steps, he gets his stride back and heads down the path. The moon is behind him, lighting his way, casting his shadow forward and to the left. He knows that means he is traveling in a certain direction, can hear his father telling him about it, but can't concentrate on it and lets it be. Not like it matters much, anyway. He has no intention of needing that information. The path should take him where he needs to go.

Reid stumbles over a large root dividing the path and takes a sudden fall to the left. His hand instinctively reaches out for support and finds the bark of a tree. It saves him from falling, the hand that caught it sliding over the coarse coating of moss and loose wood. As it does, he feels a change in the contact. Something soft protrudes from the trunk. He turns to look, eyes settling on the moonlit gaze of a boy.

It takes Reid a moment to register and another to process. The kid is as tall as he is, but looks a lot younger. His eyes are wide open, staring, glaring. There is something wrong with the front of his shirt. Reid takes in the blank stare, fingers still traveling over the boy's clothing until they come to rest on the large, dark patch over the kid's stomach. Wetness resides there. Reid pulls his hand back and looks. The liquid is black in the moonlight but has a distinctive aroma. Coppery. And now that he is paying attention, he notices another smell. A heavy and angry scent that makes his nose constrict, his stomach flutter, his mind shriek in fear even as he looks down and notices the boy's sneakers are a good foot off the ground.

The kid smells like road kill, like some squashed skunk or car-flattened raccoon left too long in the sun. Reid backs away in a hurry, slips on something slimy underfoot, stumbles and falls, not noticing the impact, eyes locked on the gaping wound in the boy's stomach. Someone is screaming into the darkness. When he realizes it's him, Reid shuts down. His own belly lurches, tries to expel something, anything, but only bile comes up. Reid hastily wipes his fingers on the ground, desperate to get the boy's blood off of him. It seems very important for some reason.

The kid is pinned to the tree trunk with what looks like big metal spikes. He dangles there, a sick and twisted art project, thought up by a madman.

Reid tries to rise, but the slick something that sent him to the ground is still stuck to his sneaker. He looks down and screams again. A length of sausage-like intestine clings to him. It drags after him like an obscene and putrid snake as he back-pedals on his hands and feet further from the dead kid. When he understands he is bringing it with him, he kicks out. The coil flies off, the contents splattering into the forest with soft, wet sounds, the flattened section landing in the middle of the path, ridged with the impression of his shoe.

Reid gasps for breath, chokes on the fresh air tainted with decay. He scrambles to his feet again, scraping his sneaker against the uneven ground, digging into the dirt of the path to get the boy's insides off of him. It isn't until he backs into a tree that his real fear kicks in.

The boy stares at him, warns him with his empty eyes, blood running in black rivers from his gut and where the spikes hold his collarbone taut. *Run*, he seems to whisper. *Run before it's too late.*

Reid can't. His body is frozen from dawning realization. The boy is dead. Dead. How, who, why, when…? The questions sputter through his mind, spin and twine around his fear and drive him to panic. But none of this matters. Not really. After the initial shock settles over him, all that really gets through to Reid is that he must be there for the same reason as this boy and that means he could be next.

The very thought drives his heart to race harder, faster, so much so he struggles to stay conscious, feeling the darkness reaching out to grab him and drag him under. He almost gives in to it, would have, he is sure of it, if it weren't for the noise.

It is nothing, really. The crack of a small branch, easily explained away by the shifting of the wind or the natural release of deadwood. But, to Reid, it is a gunshot right to his flight instinct.

He doesn't think or breathe or flinch. Instead, Reid turns and runs.

2

Reid runs until his lungs threaten to cave in. Reid runs until his ankles lose their feeling. Reid runs, the flight of a terrified animal, flinging himself forward into the unknown because he has no other choice and simply isn't able to stop himself.

Reid runs until he can't anymore. His body betrays him at last, the exertion too much for his weakened state. He staggers to a halt in the near dark of the path, barely catching himself from falling over as his equilibrium rushes to keep up with the rest of him. He collapses forward, hands on knees. What is left of his lungs heaves for air. Adrenaline pours through his system, sharpening his senses, driving away the last of whatever drug his kidnappers gave him that dulled his mind.

At least he can think now. But he isn't sure that's a good thing. Especially when he looks up and finds himself so exposed. What the hell is he thinking? He ducks into the trees off the path, suddenly not sure if hiding is even an option. Did that kid try to hide? If so, it didn't work out so well for him. Reid's mind continues to spin with questions he has no way of answering. Still, they are more coherent than they were before his headlong dash.

Who was that boy? Where did he come from? More importantly, who killed him? And why was he left on the path?

As a warning. Reid's brain works that much out. Of course. But why warn him at all? If he is prey for something or someone, if this is some kind of sick game and he is the target, why tip him off?

They want me afraid. More fun for the hunter.

His mind refuses to accept it. He has to be over reacting. Stuff like this just doesn't happen in real life. It's way too Hollywood. Any second now someone will show up and flash a camera in his face and laugh, telling him how stupid he looked running from a movie prop. Reid shudders from the memory of the boy's entrails. No. That was real. Too real. It isn't possible. And yet, here he is, alone and abandoned in the dark, deep in a forest he knows nothing about, left there by two men who seemed to think his luck has run out. How do they know?

He's still in shock and fights the effects, knowing it is slowing him down, keeping him stupid, forcing him to react instead of doing what he needs to do to survive. He thanks his father silently in the dark for teaching him how to handle himself in the woods.

To a point. Good old Dad never mentioned being kidnapped, dumped and hunted in the wilderness survival boot camp he made Reid run through for two weeks every summer. It had been fun, then. This is most definitely nothing like that.

Still, his father's levelheaded nature wins through and shakes Reid into some kind of calm. Enough he is able to work some things out.

I need answers. But first, I need to find out where I am and if I can get away.

It isn't much of a plan, but it makes him feel a little better. Just the idea of acting settles his mind and helps him focus. Reid turns and looks up at the moon. First thing's first. Bearings and direction. If he can figure out which way is north, he will at least be able to pick a goal and follow it consistently. Lost In The Woods 101. Basics, really. Stuff he's known most of his life. But at the moment, those basics are the only lifeline he has to cling to. Not for the last time, Reid whispers another thank you to his dead father.

His eyes register a flicker in the trees across the path. It's only the barest of movements, but it freaks him out and forces him deeper into the surrounding forest. Reid struggles for calm. He needs to focus. Everything that happens from now on is important and if he doesn't keep it together, he will die. The kid with the empty gut and the rotting entrails convinced him of that.

The flicker gets closer. Just a brief shadow passing, something darker than night moving through the trees, weaving in and out of sight. At times it disappears for so long Reid is sure it's his imagination until it shows up again. He holds his breath and eases himself low to the ground, ignoring the scratches he gets from the underbrush and the risk of poison oak or ivy, keeping to the full shadows. Every movement crushes needles, stirs the dirt at his feet, filling his nose with the smell of the forest. He does his best to be silent. After all, it could be an animal. Tons of big cats and even bears in these woods, he's sure. He desperately tries to remember what his father told him about surviving animal attacks, all the while trying to convince himself it must be some sort of carnivorous predator looking for dinner.

For some reason, he's pretty sure it isn't.

When the flickering shadow emerges from the darkness and sets foot on the path, Reid softly exhales through his mouth in a combination of fear and relief. Not an animal then. A man, dressed all in black. Reid half wishes it was some kind of wild creature. On the other hand, if it were, he might have a harder time. A bear or a mountain lion could take him out with little chance of defending himself. There is hope he might escape from a man.

Reid watches the dark figure glide silently down the path, everything about him screaming predator and he suddenly wonders if he's right to think there is any escape from this enemy. The hunter's clothing is tight to his body, right down to a full hood that covers his head but leaves his pale face exposed. Reid doesn't see any weapons. He knows that means little. Besides, it's not the man's attire that freaks Reid out the most. It's the way he moves. Every motion is so fluid Reid shudders. There is no way a man can move like that, not even the best-trained commando. There is an unnaturalness to it, more animal than human, but even beyond what a skulking cat could pull off.

Reid's panic takes him over for a heartbeat, screaming at him to get away. The man is a monster, has to be, something out of a horror novel or a scary movie, a creature that only looks like a man. Reid spends the next ten seconds being wrenched back and forth between his terror and his need to understand. He finally manages to wrestle himself back under control just as the hunter comes to a halt across from him.

Every cell in Reid's body demands he run, and now. He holds himself in check, his father's patient voice telling him over and over, never run from a predator. Always best to hide or play dead. Although supposedly making loud noises would do the trick as well, but somehow Reid doesn't think that will do him any good. The idea is so ludicrous he almost giggles from the stress. His skin vibrates with the agony of keeping still.

He has to tell himself over and over that this is just a man. Nothing special. Just very well trained. He has no way of knowing if he can outrun this hunter and hiding seems his best choice. Playing dead will only end with him being dead. Hiding is it. But his instincts are on fire and he desperately needs to put distance between them any way he can.

Sweat forms on Reid's upper lip, tricking down the corner of his mouth. Not thinking about it, he licks it away, eyes never leaving the man on the path. The dark head cocks to the side as Reid's tongue moves over his skin, as though hearing the near silent swipe of flesh on flesh. Reid freezes and holds his breath. No way. There is no way the man heard him. And yet, the dark figure turns further toward him and lifts his head. Reid hears snuffling. Impossible. Crazy. But it's the only explanation.

The man is searching for him by smell.

For a moment an irrational thought crosses Reid's mind as he crouches there in the darkness, watching the hunter come closer and closer. What if this man can help him? Reid is running only because of the boy he found. What if this man wasn't involved but is here to save him? Reid has no idea what is going on. Maybe if he cries out he will be saved. He catches himself as his weight shifts forward unbidden, his frantic mind searching for the logic in what is happening to him. He holds himself still and quiet again, battling his terror while he resists wiping the sweat from his face.

He'll hear me.

How, Reid hasn't a clue. But he knows it is true. And when the man's face turns toward the bushes where Reid hides, when he freezes on the path and focuses on Reid crouching in the shadows, though there is no way he should be able to spot anything in the heavy black, Reid is grateful he stilled that impulse.

This man is deadly. There is no question of that, no doubt. Trusting this man would be like handing himself over to the devil. For all Reid knows, that's exactly who the hunter is. And he *is* hunting. Everything about him yells it out loud despite his body's silence. There is no mistake, no misunderstanding.

And he knows Reid is there.

Run. He needs to run. But he is trapped in the underbrush. He can feel the prickle of thorns, the tug of the branches around him, as though the very forest has turned against him and will serve him up as a sacrifice to the hunter. Reid knows he might be able to escape deeper into the trees, but without light to see by he will most likely fall in his flight and be caught. He stays frozen, new indecision tearing him in half. He is unable to act as the man takes one sliding step closer, then another. It's like the battle between flight and terror cannot be won and Reid is caught in the middle with certain death only a breath away.

His heart is about to burst from it, he is certain. He needn't wait for the hunter to catch him. His own body might kill him first. But even while he thinks it, Reid is also sure of one more thing. If the man catches him, Reid will die. And no one will ever know.

Something starts out of the bushes further down the path. The sound is so sudden and loud in the stillness, Reid has to clamp both hands over his mouth to keep from crying out. His eyes immediately go to the source, expecting a deer or maybe a fox. Instead, he spots a skinny figure staggering onto the trail. It's a boy, about the same age as the other, the dead one on the tree. He stills like a terrified rabbit, face turned back toward Reid for a second before he tries to run.

He is clearly terrified.

Where the hell did he come from? Reid's mind can't keep up. No so the hunter. The man is in liquid motion without hesitation, prey in hand before the boy is able to take a step.

"Please!" The kid's voice is high-pitched and catches at the end. "Please!" Reid can see him between the man's legs, sneakers beating useless time against the ground, small fists thumping against the hunter's chest, his struggles ignored. His face is just visible in the moonlight. He looks like he's dead already, skin ghostly pale where it isn't streaked with filth, eyes sunken pits of black in the dark. "Don't kill me, please!"

The man says something. At least, Reid thinks so. It sounds partway between words and a chuckle. But the hunter can't be laughing. Can't be. Not while his arm lifts, hand raising high above his head, his intent obvious. There is nothing funny about the way he holds his body, how he clutches the boy so tightly there is no escape. The edge of a knife shines silver in the moonlight.

Reid knows what is coming. Feels his own guts wrench in sympathy and fear as he remembers the coils of intestine, the black, gaping hole in the abdomen of another boy. It can't happen again, not here, not now. And if it does, he can't be there to watch.

Reid tries to hold back but his self-preservation is somehow overridden by his need to save the kid. He yells, surges forward, tries to get to them but he is too late as the knife descends with startling speed.

The boy screams, his cry driving Reid's panic to take over control of his mind. As the shriek ends abruptly, sighing to an endless gurgle, Reid spins and bolts down the path, instinct finally winning over valor, the sound of the strange boy's death urging him on.

3

Reid's mind repeats a mantra as he runs. *This can't be happening. This. Can't. Be. Happening.* It won't stop running as much as his body won't stop, driving itself into his psyche over and over again as his legs piston up and down, sneakers pounding over the trail. And yet, he knows it is as real as the rocks and fallen leaves sliding under his racing feet, as the moon shining down on him, and the pine-scented wind forcing itself in and out of his aching lungs.

A headlong sprawl forces him to stop. His knees are suddenly on fire, palms aching from the impact, mouth clogged with decaying leaves and dirt. Reid spits out the mess, rolling over on his side. Whimpering in terror, he drags himself into the trees again and scans the path behind for signs of the hunter. Nothing. No one. Not even a hint of movement. Reid doesn't trust his eyes. Or any of his other senses. How can he when the one who pursues him moves like liquid lightning, as silent as the wind? Whoever the man is, he looks normal on the outside but instinctually feels like a wild animal, only better. Smarter. Able to reason and react with human instinct and cunning. Reid has no doubt the hunter can and will find him and attack without warning.

He can't think about the boy. Either of the boys, for that matter. They haunt him, but he needs to think of himself. Reid slams that reality into his consciousness until he really believes it. There are others like him out here. He has no way of knowing how many. And they are dying, just like he will die if he doesn't get the hell out of there somehow.

He still feels responsible. And guilty. The first boy gapes at him in his mind while the second one screams, "Please!" in an endless cry for help. It's almost enough to drive him mad.

Instead, he decides to run. But when he tries to go on, his body refuses to move. Both legs give out on him, his ankles throbbing from the fall. Reid is unable to run for the moment. He hugs himself in the dark, knees to his chest, making himself as small as possible while he fights off the horrors he witnessed. He manages to quiet the panting protests being torn from his throat and rocks back and forth on his haunches while his gaze scans the path and the trees around him over and over again in a never-ending cycle of fear, guilt and shame.

He should have saved that kid. He could have. If he had just moved faster, been smarter. This shouldn't be happening. Why is it happening?

That leads his aching head down a fresh path. How did he get here? Memory flickers over the past at last, taking him to the time before he was kidnapped. Before he was dropped in hell. He is relieved to let go of the death cries and the accusing stare of the dead boy's eyes.

Reid is able to recall the day before and cling to it. Or *was* it the day before? His concept of time is lost in the face of what is happening to him.

Lucy. The restaurant, so fancy he felt like an intruder in his jeans and hoodie. Her choice and her treat. She acted like she owned the place and no one said a word. They celebrated. He remembers. She finally managed to get him out of foster care. A whole year he spent after the tragic deaths of their parents, living in someone else's house, at the mercy of the state, while his twenty-year-old sister struggled to get her own life together.

He honestly never thought she would, was positive he would be in state care until he was eighteen. Not only that, Reid was sure she forgot him until the very day she came to pick him up. He was so shocked when his foster mother called him downstairs, to see Lucy standing there at the door, holding the paperwork that set him free. The smile on her face reminded him why he loved her. All his resentment disappeared. She looked good, smelled good when she hugged him, body thinner than he remembered, her blonde hair much lighter than his tickling his face as she squeezed him so hard he choked.

He didn't care. He hugged her back. And took in her new life. Her car was expensive, her clothes designer, hair and makeup flawless. She looked like a model. Or a famous actress.

"We're set up now, baby brother." She smiled at him past her big, dark sunglasses and patted his knee as he settled his hastily packed bag in the back seat of her black convertible, the combination of new car smell and freshly dyed leather making him nauseated. "Found a good job, a great boss. Set *up*."

He hadn't asked her why she didn't contact him that long year they were apart. Why she didn't call, write, email. It didn't matter. They were together.

Reid swipes at a thin tear tracing down his cheek. He doesn't have time to feel sorry for himself. Lucy. Where is his sister?

"Mr. Syracuse," Lucy said as she pulled up to their new building. It looked expensive. "Mr. Syracuse," she repeated as she led Reid onto the well-appointed elevator that streamed soft muzak at him. "Mr. Syracuse," Lucy whispered as she smiled at him and unlocked the door to their apartment. "He's great, Reid. You'll like him. He's got big plans for me. And he can't wait to meet you."

The place was posh, plush. She loved showing him around. Nice furniture, great kitchen, a bathroom Mom would have died for. And his room was huge, stocked full of clothes, too. He had his own TV, a brand new iPad. How did she get so lucky? This was way better than anything they had when their parents were alive.

He wanted to ask the cost of it all, what the real price was beyond the money it took to buy, but that was the natural cynic in him. His father's influence. Still, he wondered if his sister got herself in over her head. But he was too happy to be with her to go there just yet.

Is this the price? Reid's terror is suddenly not just for himself. His sister. She has to be out here too, somewhere. There is no way she will survive without him. Reid's panic is so strong it drives him to his feet again. His mind races. He has to find her. She's all he has, he's all she has. He refuses to lose her again.

But as he spins in place and his mind desperately searches around as though he'll find her right there with him, his heart cracks down the middle. He has no way of finding her. She could be dying right now at the hands of the hunter and there is nothing Reid can do to stop it. He hates the feeling of being worthless. He had enough of that in foster care, shuffled from one house to the next, treated like he was an inconvenience at best, a burden and a waste of skin at worst. His father taught him better than that, to respect himself, and he clung to that the whole year he waited for Lucy to come get him.

Standing there, desperate to find his sister, Reid feels his will crumple at last as it never has before. There are no options. He is lost and alone with a man out there hunting him and kids like him. Reid has no doubt if Lucy comes in contact with the hunter, she won't last a moment.

He slams one hand into the closest tree and swears softly. The pain is enough to bring him to his senses.

I need a plan. Easier thought of than done. Still. It is something to focus on and he needs that very much right now.

Reid resumes his crouch, finding the darkest shadow he can as his mind searches for a way out.

It triggers another memory.

He had been in bed, the comfortable mattress a far cry from the lumpy, musty things he'd spent the past year sleeping in. Funny how every foster home had the same kind of bed. He was stuffed with good food and a beer his sister let him drink. Lucy even tucked him in, he remembers it clearly. She smiled down at him, kissed his forehead just like Mom used to. Told him she loved him.

So what the hell happened? He was sleeping. The door slammed open in the dark, the whole apartment deep as pitch. Reid struggled, remembers fighting, but there were large shadows in the night, stronger than him and something fell on his face, pressed to his nose and mouth. It stank. He sank into quiet to the sound of Lucy screaming.

Reid shudders and pulls himself from the memory, the pit of his stomach rolling over slowly once. It is true, then. She is out there with him. This Syracuse she mentioned, he has to be in on it. Sold them to some sicko maybe? Some freak who hunts people for fun. Reid's anger surges and for a moment it gives him power. But it isn't as strong as his fear. It has only enough energy to drive him to his feet one last time.

He has to find his sister. She was always the weak one, the brittle flower, just like their mother. At least, that was what Dad always said and Reid believed him at the time. Nothing Lucy did up until now gave him reason to doubt either. And Dad would want Reid to find her and keep her safe if possible. Even though he was years younger, Reid always looked out for her as best he could.

Indecision is agony. How? Where does he go now? And where is Lucy? Reid has no answers, no hope, no direction. He has only his fear and the path before him. For a moment he gives in to the despair, wishing he is safe and she never came to get him. Fury wakes suddenly, while he blames Lucy, knowing this is all her fault.

That doesn't last long. He has never been vindictive or known to hold a grudge. And his sister is all he has. Instead, he chooses to act.

He has only one choice and he knows it. Keep moving. Search for her. And stay alive. If he can. If only long enough to protect her. Again, if he can. He knows the chances of locating her in this vast wilderness are slim. Worse than that, probably impossible. But Reid clings to the idea of finding Lucy, uses it as his means of moving forward, his motivation for staying alive.

He does one last visual check of the trail, holding his breath to listen as well. It remains empty, the night quiet and calm. He weighs his options. He can go back the way he came, on the chance the hunter moved on and perhaps left something useful behind, or he can keep going forward. Reid checks the moon. It is falling across the sky, setting behind him. Which means it must be headed west. He knows that much. He studies the path again. To return the way he came will take him south. The path continues to the north. Not that it matters. But his is an orderly mind and Reid finds small comfort in knowing at least what direction he is headed.

He can't bring himself to go back. It would mean finding the remains of the second boy, possibly in the same position he found the first. He isn't sure his sanity can survive that. Besides, as long as he moves forward, there is hope, as slim as that dream is.

When his sneakers touch the path, he is already turned the opposite way, frightened gaze watching everything around him as his steady footfalls carry him deeper into the forest.

4

It is a struggle to use logic, but the longer Reid goes without being challenged the easier it is to forget from moment to moment what is happening around him. He can't block it out completely and when he remembers after a few seconds respite, it's a jolt to his already stressed system. And yet he cherishes each and every scrap of peace such delusions bring.

He knows there is no future for him in running around like a terrified animal. He has to get himself together. Having a plan, a goal he can take steps toward even in times when he is afraid and just needs to run is the only way he will win his freedom. After he breaks out, he will allow himself to fall apart again. But for now, he has to keep moving and pay attention.

And be careful. Not that there is any worry he will drop his constant vigilance, not yet. He feels himself waning, but not enough for it to slip completely. There is simply too much at stake. His own life, yes. And Lucy's. Always his need to find Lucy, sitting on him like a burden, keeping him pointed in the direction he chose.

Reid's mind wanders around his problems, feeding the questions he has no answers for with doubt and the seeds of anger. Why them? Why the boy who died on the tree, the one who was killed on the path? Why himself and his helpless sister who didn't know when she was being conned? No one to miss them, he supposes. Parents dead, grandparents, too. Maybe it's the same for the other kids. Would have to be. No aunts and uncles. Just him and his sister and those lost ones he wishes he could forget.

Easy targets.

He tries to muster outrage. It would be preferable to the terror. Even some self-righteous anger would serve him. But Reid can't get much past his constant fear, even getting comfortable in it, letting it settle around him like a family heirloom. For him. For the unknown kids he left behind. And for Lucy.

What about the hunter? Reid can only assume he is some kind of serial killer because his mind can't process much past the expected. Either that or a rich guy with a taste for gutting people. Reid is pretty sure money can buy even that if the right amount is involved. The right people. Again his thoughts turn to Lucy's new boss. The more he thinks about it, the more Reid is sure the asshole sold them out.

Still, his anger stays away, only a dull and deliberate regret filling the space between panic and terror. But he is able to at least plot revenge and that helps him pass the time. It distracts him too, so he forces himself to drop that line of thinking. He can't afford to let his mind wander.

Instead, he dives into the list of practical things he needs to survive, the tools his father taught him were important if he was ever lost in the woods. Mind you, he is certain Dad never foresaw anything like the situation Reid finds himself in. His father used to tease about that side of him, how he always wanted a plan no matter what he walked into. But Dad always said it with a sense of pride so Reid knew he was doing right.

Too bad Mom and Dad weren't more like their son. Then their deaths wouldn't have left him in foster care and his fragile sister unable to get her life together without going to work for some sick freak who sold them into a death sentence.

That's better. The glimmer of anger is his at last. There is more energy in it than the fear, but just as much focus.

He pauses by a crumbling spruce tree. The top half leans at a crazy angle, boughs hanging to the ground, its weight bending the trunks of those it presses on. It forms a thick barrier that completely blocks the path. Reid approaches with caution, mind screaming at him not to go anywhere near it, to turn around and run the other way. His heart rate climbs dramatically until he eases close enough to see the trunk has snapped by nature, not designed as a trap by the hunter. The tree is old and fell on its own, but its presence still forces him to leave the trail and go around.

Reid struggles through the underbrush and considers his course. He has already discarded the idea of traveling straight through the forest. It's just too dark and there are too many unknowns. The ground is uneven here, full of emerging tree roots and bulging rocks hidden in the undergrowth, just waiting for him to trip and fall over them. And for all he knows there are worse things he's not seeing, gaps and chasms and deep holes his mind conjures to torment him. He could end up hurt or unconscious from a fall into such a place, a broken ankle or cracked skull spelling the end of him.

In that case, the hunter wouldn't need to kill him. Mother Nature would do her own job of it.

Still, when he sets foot back on the path, he wonders how long he can risk staying out in the open like this. He is sure the trail is there for a reason, like a rabbit trap line, set along their own run. It may be the logical road to take, but that sword cuts both ways. How simple is it for the hunter to use these paths, the ideal tracking ground?

He doesn't want to make things too easy for the man, but Reid is tired and has other priorities before he can consider breaking away from the trail.

First things first. Water, shelter, food. Reid spent enough time in the woods camping with Dad to know what he needs to do to survive. He has as yet to stumble over a water source, or even somewhere that seems safe to hide long enough to rest. Part of him is praying for morning and light, that same part whispering he'll be safe when the sun comes up, that the hunter won't chase him in the daytime. Reid has no idea if he's right, but clings to the shred of hope and hangs onto it like it's the only thing he has.

Which, really, it is.

He is so focused and feeling in control that when a branch behind him breaks with an echoing snap he is shocked to find himself running full out down the path, panting all over again, his terror making his feet move before his mind can register what happened. And try as he might, Reid is unable to stop himself. In fact, he allows the fear to control him, giving over to it completely. He hurtles down the rutted trail at horrible speed, feet pounding loudly over the packed dirt, arms pumping at his sides, wind whistling from his lips, his animal instincts driving him forward without thought or consideration.

It feels good to give in, to release his control and let go, but the more he does, the worse his fear gets. Speed and headlong flight increases his terror exponentially until his heart is ready to explode. It's as though the hunter breathes on his neck, driving his feet faster and faster until Reid's breaths are sobs of terror and gasps for air all at once.

All the while, hovering before his eyes, his memory forcing him to look, is the vacant face of the dead boy in the tree. It is an inescapable image locked into his fear, mocking him for his flight, laughing at him, welcoming him to the family of the dead.

His foot catches and the ground rushes up to meet him. This time when Reid falls he stays where he is, knees aching from the impact with the ground, face on fire where his cheek slapped the harsh surface of the trail. He coughs out into the dust and debris floating around him and simply lays there, sprawled with arms and legs outstretched, waiting for what is to come, unable to run another step.

His eyes settle on a low, dense pile of underbrush. His self-preservation urges him to roll over once, twice and into the mass, wriggling himself inside, ignoring the pokes and prods and jabs of the plants and shrubs as they tug at his skin and clothing. The scent of disturbed earth and crushed greenery is a dead giveaway, he is sure. Reid allows one last choking sob and stills, unable to do anything about it, and even closes his eyes for a moment.

Whatever is to come, he has run as far as he can, as fast as he can. If death is right behind him, he has done his best. His eyes droop, close over and he loses himself to the darkness.

Reid starts awake, amazed he was able to fall asleep at all, considering. One look at the moon, low and swollen on the horizon, tells him he did, and for at least an hour. He isn't sure what woke him, but decides it's time to move. Whether he needs more rest or not, staying in one place too long just doesn't seem safe. As he shifts and shimmies his way to the edge of the shrubs, he freezes, terror in his throat, right at the back of his mouth, choking him.

Was that a sound? An owl offers a sleepy *whoo.* He holds his breath, listening with all his might, with every cell and sense. A branch cracks, settles. A soft wind rustles the leaves of the trees, rubbing the spruce needles together, creating a soft patter as dried bits fall to the forest floor around him, raining him with debris. He swats at the pieces that land in his hair, fear driving him to it.

He holds himself steady, waits a little longer, still listening, heart falling back to normal speed. Reid knows he can't afford to panic again. Another fall like the one that sent him here and he could sprain an ankle or break something and then he would be lost for sure. Bad enough he is afraid of the forest. The relative smoothness of the trail shouldn't be so hard. But he is tired and impulsive and that makes it easy to lose control. Above all else he has to get his control back. If only because he needs his body whole and in good health if he is going to survive.

Why he expects to survive or even considers it an option he doesn't know, but it refuses to leave him, that idea, and he doesn't have the heart to chase it away.

Reid is startled and crippled when his stomach cramps with hunger, a fist of pain and nausea driving through his gut all the way to his spine. He clutches at his waist, arms hugging his abdomen, unable to do anything about it. All of a sudden it feels like he hasn't eaten for days, as though his body has turned against him and is literally cannibalizing itself. He wonders how long he was in the custody of the men who left him here. Only the passage of time would explain the emptiness inside him.

A long and wrenching howl echoes in the distance. Reid is familiar with many animals, thanks to his time with his father camping. He's heard the cries of wolves and coyotes, the uncanny human screams of foxes, the grunting snuffles of passing bears. Never before has he heard anything like the alien shriek carrying over the trees and through them, reaching for him, clutching at his heart and soul. It freezes him in place, blanking his mind, emptying him of thought and all feeling but pure and crippling terror.

He would have laid there and waited for whatever it was to come and get him. But his attention is broken. He jerks around to see a girl dart from her place across the path from him and tear off down the trail in the same direction he has been running.

Away from that sound.

Reid hesitates no longer. His fear releases him so he can start running again. A sudden need to be with another human being drives him forward and on her trail, determined to get what answers he can.

5

Reid's instincts know there is only one reason the girl would be running and understands she's just made herself a target. But she is close, so close, and the chance to talk to someone else, to compare notes and maybe get some answers, is just too powerful for him to ignore.

He catches her easily, his longer legs chasing her down. She spots him, her features just visible in the last of the moonlight. She looks as terrified as he feels, her eyes huge and glistening, mouth hanging open as she pants for breath. She looks about his age but older somehow, almost ancient. Reid reaches for her to make her stop. It's uncanny how she dodges him, forcing her way deeper into the trees.

He is so shocked he almost stops in his tracks. Obviously she's been running for a while, has learned something from her ordeal. She is wily and he wonders how long it took her to get to this animal place of pure survival. He takes notes without meaning to, pays attention to how she moves, hoping her tactics will keep him alive, too.

The underbrush is sparse here, the trees themselves thinning and leaving gaps easier to run through. The ground is rockier as well, more moss and stone than dirt and far more treacherous than he would like. Reid remembers his last fall and wonders if the pursuit is worth it. But his need won't let him stop, committing him to the chase. He paces her, wanting to call out but too worried the sound of his voice will carry, though he knows their retreat is making almost as much noise as any words would.

There is no way he is letting her escape. He has a sudden thought and can't seem to let it go. As he rolls it around in his mind, he knows he is right. They are weaker on their own, easy pickings. If he had someone to watch his back he could rest, and give his partner a turn. They could make plans, work out their strategy together. Just being with someone else could make such a difference. And why stop at two? There is strength in numbers, just like in school when bullies come calling. Loners get trashed while groups are safe.

They need to stick together and do what they can to find more like them.

Besides, he has to talk to her, to hear another voice. Before he can even make a move toward her again she swerves, stumbles and catches herself, spinning and going the other way just as his fingers brush over the coarse fabric of her sweater. She reminds him of a fleeing rabbit, all reaction and instinct. He doesn't want to have to hunt her down, the very thought disgusts him, but she's not giving him a choice. He worries expending so much energy chasing her will tire him out for when the real running starts again. He knows that could happen at any time, especially if her reason for bolting is what he thinks it is. He briefly considers dropping the whole idea and continuing on himself, but can't shake the feeling that he needs her and she needs him.

Reid swears very softly and turns after her.

For a moment he loses her in the forest and quickly comes to a halt. He tries to hold his breath despite his straining lungs, his ears serving him better than his eyes in the dark. Just as he is forced to take a breath, he catches the rustle of leaves and a soft sigh of air. Reid spins toward the sound and sees a hint of movement while the pungent smell of body odor laced with musty dirt reaches his nose, so strong he can taste it in the back of his throat. His mind flickers to the memory of the hunter sniffing the air and Reid understands.

No wonder the man was using his nose. The scent is unmistakable. It oozes human suffering and despair.

Reid is about to go to her when he sees the leaves shudder. He knows it's her, that she caused the movement, but still he panics, that response too natural now to avoid. He creeps up behind her, not wanting to scare her, but not knowing how else to get to her without her running off again.

Reid needn't have worried. She glares at him, baring her teeth, her cheeks wet, and tries to shoo him off, flapping her hands at him, but no longer trying to get away. Her sweater bags off of her narrow shoulders, face filthy, tangled hair a halo of leaves around her head. Deep lines etch her cheeks, filled with dirt. Her eyes are sunken far into their orbits and they glare at him like he is the hunter himself.

He was wrong about her age. Reid thought she was sixteen or so. But up close he gets a better look and his whole being lurches in sympathy.

He's sure she's no more than twelve years old.

Reid tucks in beside her and presses his mouth to her ear, flinching from the stink of her skin, his voice barely a breath, just loud enough so she can hear.

"We can help each other."

She jerks back from him and tries to wiggle around, but he holds her easily with one hand. She relaxes for a heartbeat, looking up into his eyes. The moisture on her face isn't sweat like he thought it was. She's sobbing silently and all her humanity is leaking out with her tears.

"Let me go." She huddles there in his power, soul empty of all but her fright and the knowledge she is about to die. He can see there is little left of the girl he knows she had to be once, before the horror took over. It makes him want to scream. And worry it could happen to him. Will happen. He refuses to believe it is inevitable.

"How long have you been running?" It's important to him. He needs to know what the limit is, how much of his own life is left if he can compare it to hers.

"Four days." She snuffles very softly, wiping at her nose with her sleeve. "Like you give a crap."

He is hurt, the truth of it driving into his already wounded heart. When it settles over him, his grief numbs. Of course she feels that way. Alone out here for four whole days by herself?

"How did you survive?" She amazes him. He's barely made it through one night.

"I'm smart." She is limp, but he can feel her tension now, the hum of it that runs through her. She is ready to move at the first opportunity. "And small. Guess they like bigger targets more than me."

"I'm Reid." It also feels important she knows his name.

She shrugs. "Monica." Her eyes flicker around them in a calculated pattern. "Don't think I trust you now."

Fair enough. "Didn't ask you too," he says.

"Did," Monica's eyes come back to his. "You said we could help each other. Well, I've heard that before."

Someone found her and abandoned her. It is the only explanation. How can he convince her he'd never leave her behind when he doesn't know he wouldn't? Nothing is sure anymore. And if the chance came up to rescue Lucy, he knows he'll choose his sister over what remains of this little girl. Still, he lets the outrage of it show in his face.

"I'm sorry." It's not much, but it seems to work on her. She shivers and sighs deeply, her tension going quiet for the moment.

"Not your fault," she says, "or theirs. Just, I'm younger and slower and they couldn't wait for me. I get it." She snuffles for the second time, her sleeve now dark from cleaning up her tears. "But it's still not fair."

He's been thinking the same. No such thing as fair in this place. Would he do what they others did? Run off without her? Would he let her hold him back? In that moment, he decides. No matter what happens, he'll protect her if he can.

"I'm not them," he says. "Will you come with me?"

Maybe if he reached her a day earlier or even before darkness fell. But he can feel her need overthrown by her fear of rejection, that instant of wanting to be part of something washed over in her eyes by her own instinctual drive not to trust him.

"We can't stay here." Monica tries to pulls free but he won't release her. It would mean letting go of the hope he had that they could run together. Still, he agrees with her. They have to move. Maybe if they find somewhere safer he can change her mind.

"That cry." Reid shudders.

"They're coming." She gives another gentle tug and he finally lets her go. Monica sits up, but doesn't run away. It's a start at least.

"What are they?" He knows he should let her run. There isn't much in her anymore. But he can't just let her go. She reminds him so much of Lucy for some reason, it would be like losing his sister all over again.

Monica shakes her head, her filthy hair dropping a few leaves. "I don't know."

"How did you get here?" His desperation is rising, tied to hers.

"I don't know." Her words are breathed around a silent sob.

"Why are they doing this?"

"I don't know. I don't know. *I don't know*!" She might as well be screaming. Her whole being *is* screaming, shaking him up even though her frustration and fear is expressed at a whisper. Her face crumples and her little fists beat against him, her skinny body wriggling back and forth.

"Shut up. I don't care. It doesn't matter. Just shut up!" She hisses at him like a small animal, her tiny hands now claws, slashing toward his face, his chest. "You'll bring them here!"

He barely has a moment to realize what she said. For the second time. Them. What does she mean, *them*? Reid hasn't even considered there could be more than one hunter. He is so overwhelmed by this news he almost misses her sudden reaction to something he hasn't heard.

She tenses, a frightened rodent, cheek twitching convulsively in terror. A low and horrible hum rises from her stomach, coming up to her chest and out through the flare of her nostrils. She twists in Reid's grip, trying to slide free. He wants to hang onto her, but he is stunned, made useless by what she told him, so he lets her go. When she pulls away and glances at him, he finally understands. They have nothing to offer one another after all. She is simply too far gone.

Still, Reid doesn't want to leave her there. He can help her get to a safer place before they part ways. Before he can act, she moves two steps and locks up again. He is about to urge her to move when he feels it. They are not alone. He searches their surroundings, slinking slowly and carefully into the depth of the shadow she just left. There, near the path. Something moves with deliberate slowness. Reid sees Monica tremble. She hasn't moved. And needs to, quickly. She only has a moment. He reaches for her, too late. She uncoils from her fearful freeze and dashes several steps toward the trail.

The hunter is there in one fluid motion, snatching her out of the brush with a whoosh of air, dropping her into the open. Reid hears her scrawny body thud to the dirt, the gasp of escaping breath as she loses hers. Reid is forced to press his hands over his ears as her low hum begins again, turning into a piercing keen so loud it shakes him to his bones with its desperation.

There. Beside the hunter. A form slides from the darkness. Another one. Them, she said. *Them.* She was right. Two hunters. Two killers in the night.

He didn't want to believe her. Now he has no choice. She's proved it to him in the worst way possible. His horror growing, Reid forces himself to move on, to escape the sound and Monica's final torment. Her death.

He has gone less than ten steps when her humming protest, the last weapon she has in a terribly unbalanced war, is cut off abruptly. Forever.

Reid runs.

6

This time he runs without reason, his focus lost to him, as much an animal as she was in the end. He finds the edge of the trail and hates to use it, but has no choice, instinct forcing him to take the path of least resistance. He must run and run and never, ever stop. Not for anything or anyone. Rest is impossible, brief moments caught in jerking instances of gasping air, barely enough to restore his wind before he is off again, a new sound or flicker of motion chasing him deeper and deeper into the forest.

He only peripherally feels the ground under his feet, the slap of branches against his face when he gets too close to the edge of the trees, usually after he spins to check the trail behind him. Reid can't think or feel or reason. He doesn't have time and can't afford the effort any of them take. He is legs and feet, ragged breath and burning muscle, sheathed in a world of pain and terror driving him onward, ever onward.

He has only a heartbeat to register the barrier before he reaches it, but it is just enough to keep him from hurtling headlong into the chain link fence. He stops all at once, whole body twitching in response, gaping upward, feeling his skin tingle and the hair on his head and body stand on end in answer to the power running through it. The dull metal thrums a steady beat, vibrating its way down into the ground. Reid doesn't need to check or even think about it. He just knows.

There is enough juice running through the fence to kill him.

Reid is so stunned by its appearance and obvious meaning, it takes him a while to react to it. His flight mode has been interrupted and he is so tired and strung out from stress and fear it takes him achingly long moments to register and understand what is going on. When he finally gets it, he wants to fall to his knees and quit. On top of everything else, whoever dumped him here has trapped him as well. The unfairness of it shrivels his soul a little further and he spends a moment rubbing at the gooseflesh raised by the electricity and his own despair. Until he considers the fence again. And a ray of hope shines through.

It has to have a gate. Maybe more than one. If he can find the way out… nothing will keep him from escaping.

Without Lucy? His mind tortures him with the thought.

Of course not. But knowing where the way out is will be a great advantage when he does find her. Reid refuses to think about the alternative. He knows there is a chance she has already met with her fate at the hands of the hunter. Hunters. He shudders again, backing off a bit from the fence. How many are there, then? He was obviously wrong thinking there is only one man. He sees how foolish that assumption was, but only in hindsight. There was no way he could have even for a moment believed there was more than one of those men. It took seeing it to believe it. Now that he *has* seen two, his mind swells with horrible possibility. There could be dozens. Hundreds. They could have him surrounded right now.

Reid spins and checks the forest around him. As far as he can tell, he is alone. When he returns his attention to the problem of the fence, he has recovered more of himself and the focus he lost in his overwhelmed flight.

There is only one way to find the way out if this idea of his could be his salvation or not. He has to follow the fence. Reid looks back and forth, first one way then the other, trying to decide. On his left the fence curves off into the darkness, barely visible in the thickening trees. But on his right, where the forest is thinner, he can see more of it up ahead. He chooses that way, only because he is tired and the ground seems less treacherous, the cover not so stifling. And while he knows he trades ease of movement with shelter from the hunters, Reid trusts his gut and goes to the right.

West, he corrects himself. *I'm going west.* That's almost the deal breaker for him. He would rather head toward the dawn and see the sun lighting the sky, leading him into the morning. In fact, he's looking forward to it. And yet, he sticks with his plan and trudges on.

Reid sets out, stepping gingerly over the body of a dead rabbit, barely a day gone, flies humming their ravenous dance over it. He forces his eyes away, not wanting to contemplate what would have happened to him if he hadn't stopped.

It isn't worth thinking about.

He finds it hard to focus on the world on his side of the fence. His eyes scan the other, for a sign, a chance of rescue, anything. Anyone. It's such a thin barrier, really. Such a simple yet effective wall between him and freedom. It drives him a bit mad when he focuses on it and he has to look away from time to time or fall back into spiraling despair. He fantasizes about coming across someone, a forest ranger maybe. A logging truck. But there is only the forest, the night and the quiet to keep him company. Those and the constant buzz of the fence.

It annoys him after a short time, even though he longs for it and what it means. Civilization. People. Safety. The very things he treasures, powered by the only thing keeping him from his life.

Despite the brief sleep he caught a few hours ago, Reid is stumbling tired, his legs barely able to keep him upright. So, when he hears a car horn he thinks he is hallucinating. His eyes see the lights in the distance, register the sight, but don't translate what they mean for a long time. When he finally realizes what he is looking at, his heart leaps up and jerks him toward the fence. He is again wide awake.

There are cars in the distance. Their tires rumble over asphalt, a steady rush and hum as they pass. Trucks roll by, powered with their distinctive roar. Brightness cuts through the dark, makes paths across the trees, sending shadows bouncing in steady streams only to die and be reborn from the next set of headlights.

The highway vibrates with steady life, not even a mile in the distance. He is elevated, looking down on it, the passing interstate in some kind of shallow valley below him. He can almost smell the gasoline fumes, the heat from the engines. He is sure he hears music echoing in the distance from someone's open window.

He wants to shout, jump up and down and laugh all at once. This is it, what he's been searching for! Until he works out the final part of the situation in his exhausted and fuzzy head. And when he does, he wishes he never saw the fence or the cars or the people going on with their lives while he remains trapped with the monsters.

There is no exit here. The interstate is too far for the moving cars to hear him. He has no way of signaling that he is in trouble. For a moment he has a fresh rush of hope. A fire! He could set a fire. Surely someone would come. But he has nothing to make a fire with, no matches or lighter and is sure he can't do it the old fashioned way. He tried and tried as a child after his father told him native people used to kindle flames from a pair of sticks. All he ever managed to do was give himself splinters.

Reid stands there for a long time, forgetting the hunters and his fear and gives in to his longing. Safety is so close he can smell it, taste it, feel the end of his terror and pain. He is almost desperate enough, tempted by the thought of that highway in the distance, to just risk it and touch the fence. Maybe he will survive? But reason explains to him very gently even if he does, he will only make it to the fence itself and will never manage to get over the top with all that power running through him.

He doesn't want to abandon his only glimmer of hope, but has to face the truth at last. Reid can't just stay there. It's too dangerous. He finally trudges onward, still following the fence, easing his disappointment by trying to convince himself there must be another spot just like this one, closer to the road even. A place he can call for help.

Small consolation. Smaller still as he passes through a line of trees. He hesitates one last moment, absorbing the hint of humanity in the distance before pushing himself onward.

The last of the sound and light from the highway is lost behind him.

He isn't aware he is crying until his vision swims in front of him and he is forced to wipe at his eyes with the filthy cuff of his hoodie. Reid chokes, spitting out precious moisture, his throat so thick and painful he can't bring himself to swallow.

The night seems to last forever. He wonders if it will ever end. It's like he's been dropped into a wilderness of darkness and despair that goes on and on forever.

He keeps the fence in sight and feeling, using it to guide him. It isn't until he stumbles over a loose stone that he realizes the trees are almost gone. Reid slows and looks around. He has left the scant comfort and security of the forest behind and stands on a low cliff face. The fence lines the edge, the rest lost to him. Reid gets as close as he can and peers over the side. He feels his foot slip, the stone crumbling beneath him and for a moment he is sure he is gone. He cries out as his sneaker slides out from under him, throwing himself to the ground. A patter of stones fall, nearly dragging him to his death against the fence. He catches his breath, holding it, listening. It is a long and quiet moment before the stones hit the bottom.

Reid hastily backs off and gives the fence more room. He keeps his distance, watching his step more carefully. The trees return, sparse at first, slowly thickening and embracing him again. Reid tries to stay in sight of the fence, but the terrain is just too dangerous, the trees too thick. Still, he keeps his eyes locked on it.

He knows he is going down before he feels the pain in his leg, but is unable to stop himself. Reid's ankle protests the abuse it's taken, finally giving up on him over the loose stone that sends him to his knees. He breathes hard, massaging his foot, hoping he hasn't done much damage. A tentative try of his weight tells him he's in luck. This time.

With great regret, Reid finally lets the fence go. His heart abandons him, leaving only hurt and horror behind. He can't explain to himself why, but seeing the last glimmer of the chain link and shedding the feeling of its power is like losing his best friend.

He angles deeper into the forest and almost immediately stumbles across a pathway. He pauses at the edge, thinking and listening while his body aches and begs him for rest. Reid briefly considers trying to erect some kind of camouflaged shelter, but discards the idea just as fast. Not like he'd get any rest anyway. His best bet is to keep moving. And, if possible, get to a gate in the fence.

As he sets foot on the path, he looks up and to the right, into the blush of dawn lighting the sky.

7

At least one thing is in his favor, Reid figures. He was right about direction. And the sun is very, very welcome in his dark and terrible new world. The light lifts his spirits somewhat, easing the tension inside him enough that he actually has the illusion he is safe for moments on end. He knows it isn't smart to lose his edge, but he has been running all night and needs those stolen moments to keep him from falling apart.

Still, he is emotionally and physically exhausted, crippled by hunger and thirst. Both have gotten worse as time goes on and he knows his need for water must be satisfied soon or he risks delirium and collapse.

He is drawn thin and once he adjusts to the idea of morning and loses his sense of hope, the brightening sky turns on him, only makes him feel more transparent and unreal.

As the light of dawn washes over his weary body, a secret part longs for the return of the black and quiet of night.

With the morning comes more sound than he is used to. Birds, small animals, insects all rise and greet the day. After the stillness of the night, punctuated only by the occasional passing creature outside the horror he witnessed, the new day wakes to a cacophony of nature. The birds are the worst, their happy songs piercing his eardrums, giving him a headache and stirring his fury. Reid stoops at one point and retrieves a rock, firing it at a happily chirping robin. The red-breasted bird flies off with a non-musical squawk of protest that makes Reid smile for some reason.

When he hears the gushing, burbling sound of water running he surges forward to greet it. This sound is welcome. More than welcome. He staggers through a line of trees to the edge of the rushing stream. Reid slides over the wet rocks that make its bed and falls to his knees next to it, plunging his face into the icy flow without a moment's hesitation. He gulps mouthful after glorious mouthful, his cheeks numb after the initial shock, dehydrated body greedy for more than his stomach can handle. Reid falls back onto the bank with a moan of pleasure, collapsing on the polished stones with an almost musical clatter, clutching his distended belly and wishing he could fit the whole of the stream inside him.

The cramps are inevitable and he accepts them with only a minor flinch of regret. Most of the water surges back up and out of him in a gush that makes his ribs ache and his throat even more raw than it was before he drank. Reid waits until the heaving is through and returns to the water. This time he goes slowly, forcing himself to take only a mouthful, sitting back to roll its lovely coldness around his tongue, feeling the zing of it against the fillings in his molars. He swallows after a ten count and waits another five seconds before taking another drink. And another. He waits each time, making sure the last will stay with him before risking the next and grateful for every single drop.

At last he is full of water, but not painfully so. He splashes some more on his face and blots his skin with the corner of his dirty T-shirt. This is his first opportunity to get a good look at himself and he does so carefully. Someone dressed him in the clothes he had on when Lucy picked him up. He wonders about that. Reid is dismayed by the tears in his jeans, the dirt ground into the elbows and knees of his navy blue hoodie. He takes a moment to rip off a strip of his T-shirt and clean the wounds on his knees. It's not like he's never skinned them before, but not without access to medical attention. The last thing he needs is to get an infection.

When he is done, he is satisfied. The skin is pink, some scabbing over, but neither knee is hot to the touch. Any rise in temperature would be a sure sign of trouble. Reid sighs deeply at his good luck just as his eyes drift to his sneakers. They seem to be holding up all right, though something brownish stains the top of his right one. He panics as soon as he realizes it's blood, plunging his whole foot into the water to get the last remains of the boy's entrails off of him.

Reid shudders and does his best to pull himself together after that. His eyes trace the path of the stream and he knows, before making a firm decision, he has no choice but to follow it. He has yet to come across another water source and worries there might not be one. There is the concern that the hunters will know this is a prime location to search for him, but he has to take the risk. Whether they kill him or he dies of dehydration, he's just as dead.

Of course, that's how he feels now. He's pretty sure if one of the hunters shows up he will bolt for freedom and not think twice about water. Reid bends over the stream for one more drink and looks up, not knowing that very thought is about to be tested.

There. Across the dancing, happy brook that glitters in the morning sunlight, slightly down stream. A man dressed all in black crouches, watching him.

Reid's panic drives him to run while his need to survive forces him to stop and observe. There is something wrong with the way the man looks. Something odd about how he hunches in place, observing Reid. And when the black-dressed hunter lifts his head and calls out, the cry he utters is the same as the cry from the night before, that terrifying and soul-slaying howl Reid was sure came from the throat of some horrible beast.

Reid is all out of luck. He was right after all. There is no time for a second though about the stream. He runs.

The hunter is right behind him. Reid is sure of it. He can feel the man breathing against his neck, his knife brushing against Reid's lower back, just above the kidneys. His life is over all because he lost his focus over a stupid pair of sneakers. And now Reid knows daylight is no deterrent. That particular disappointment cuts deep. His only real regret is that he was unable to find and save his sister. Lucy's name is on Reid's lips as he spins to stand and face the death that is right behind him.

He is alone. Reid gasps from the truth of it. But wait. There, in the trees, just visible. The hunter. Following him, but keeping his distance. Never before has Reid felt so much like a mouse being toyed with by a stalking cat. Now he understands how it feels to be nothing, inconsequential. Something to be played with and discarded when his usefulness is done. And yet, the hunter holds off and Reid takes advantage of the fact. Knowing it is useless, that he will die when the hunter chooses to kill him, Reid turns and runs on.

These trees are just thick enough to offer cover but are sparse in undergrowth and so are easy to maneuver. Good for Reid and better for his pursuer. He wonders how much time he has left and what the hunter is waiting for.

Reid can't help himself. He glances back over his shoulder. What he sees almost drops him to his knees in terror.

There are two of them, now. As he tears his eyes away from them he hears their communication, soft chuffing and growling, more expected from the throats of animals than humans.

But they must be human. They look human, don't they? Again that feeling of wrongness washes over Reid. How can it be? They are one or the other. His logical mind refuses to bend while his fear whispers to him. Why can't they be both?

Another howl joins their chatter from the distance, off to the south. Reid's breath comes in whispered whimpers as he tries for more speed, more distance, knowing it is useless, that he is useless and nothing he can do will save his life.

One he may have outrun. Two is a slice of impossible. Three? He might as well just give up right now and let them take him. Pack animals don't quit until their quarry is dead.

He staggers through the edge of the trees and into a clearing. Reid blinks against the brightness of the sun, missing the canopy of the forest and hesitates only for a heartbeat before plunging forward. He is a deer chased by wolves, vulnerable and fragile. He knows he is exposed, but for the moment his only friend is speed and the empty meadow offers him a chance to go even faster.

Reid crashes through the tall grass, every step steeped in fear. It seemed like such a short distance when he started out, a brief and rapid way across. But the tangled meadow foliage grabs at his sneakers even more than the underbrush in the forest and he is sweating from the heat of the sun. The safety of the trees seems so far to him, he sobs once in frustration and fear. All of his focus is on the line of trees, the relative darkness of the woods and he throws himself toward it like it is his salvation.

He is suddenly over the threshold and back into the forest, his lungs ready to quit, legs quivering from strain. And yet he runs on. Reid has no choice. He strains to listen, to hear them and realizes he hasn't picked up any sound from them since he crossed the clearing. Could it be he lost them? His heart doesn't want to dare hope it is true and his mind refuses to believe.

A glance behind shows him the truth. They ease toward him, soft shadows moving like ghosts, holding back. There are three of them now. Silent because there is no longer any need to communicate. They have him and they know it. They will toy with their prey for as long as it amuses them and then they will swoop in and kill him.

Reid wants to scream, to fight back, but instead he gathers what remains of his strength and runs.

He tries to focus on moving forward, but knowing they are behind him terrifies him. Reid stumbles more often, his feet tangling in the brush and on roots. He is thinking too hard, about running, escaping and it is destroying his speed.

Reid doesn't want his end to come when he isn't looking, but he is terrified to stop and let it be over like this. His father's voice tells him he needs to face his death like a man, to stop, turn and fight for as long as he can and never, ever quit.

He looks back without thinking about it, obeying his father's words in that small way. Reid can't see them anymore, but he knows they are back there, stalking him. He scans around for something to fight with, anything, but he is moving too fast and refuses to slow until he can't run any longer. Besides, he knows he will never win this fight. He silently begs his father's forgiveness for being a coward and continues to stagger onward.

Was that a sound? Reid can barely hear above his own pounding heart and the wheezing rattle that is his breathing. They are getting closer, that must be it. They are on top of him, he is certain. Any second now a knife will bring him down and his entrails will fall to the path, his body hung lifeless as a warning to the next poor unfortunate kid to get dumped in this hell.

He risks it and scans behind him one last time. He is alone, blessedly alone. There is no sign of them, not even a glimmer. But why did they give up the pursuit? They had him, they must have known it. Did they find more delectable prey to chase? He wishes he didn't feel so happy about that idea, knowing if that is the case his salvation comes at the loss of another life.

Reid chooses his survival over compassion, at least for the moment, and spins to make a final sprinting effort.

Only to collide full on into one of the hunters.

8

Reid lashes out immediately before his tortured brain can register these men aren't dressed in black, but camo-green.

"Whoa, there, kiddo!" He is grabbed, shaken slightly. "Where's the fire?" The man who grips him is burly and broad shouldered, a massive handle bar mustache drooping to his chin. But his brown eyes are amused and there is no fear in him.

"Not exactly the game we were looking for," his friend smirks.

It is Reid's turn to grab on and not let go. The first man staggers backward a step as Reid throws himself forward, clutching at the front of the camo jacket, fingers twining in the straps and bulging pockets. He is stunned to find the men are real after all. His sense of touch proves it.

"Please!" His voice scares him, it is so high pitched.

The whine of a terrified animal. He sounds way younger than he feels. "They're going to kill me!"

Neither man moves for a moment, as though this information is some sort of spell trapping them and keeping them from the truth. In that moment, Reid feels helpless all over again, a victim without recourse. For all he knows, they are in on it.

While his panic tries to drag him away again, the first man starts to laugh.

"Kid," he says, winking at his friend, "you've got some sick sense of humor on you."

They both chuckle. Reid's jaw feels unhinged. Laughter is so foreign to him he can't take it, not for another second. How can they find humor in this? They haven't witnessed what he has seen. Does their laughter mean they don't believe him? That can't be. Not after everything he has been through. They need to believe.

"You have to help me, please, you have to." The words blurt out ahead of his silent scream for them to save him. Only then does he notice they are armed. Nice big rifles and backpacks he hopes are full of bullets. "They're right behind me." He forgot in the shock of finding the men there. His terror flings him around as Reid spins and scans the trees.

Nothing. Had they gone, then? Did he lose them after all? Reid's confusion makes him tremble and hesitate.

Still, his obvious fear has managed to stir these men to concern.

"Kid, you on something?" Mustache backs off another step, his gun slightly raised and swung in Reid's direction.

They think he is a threat, really? He has no way to defend his actions but to beg.

"Please." He feels tears rise, his hands trembling from the effort it takes to make them understand. "You have to believe me." They just have to.

The men exchange a look. Reid can feel their lingering doubt but they swing their guns forward now, away from him, and look more alert.

"I know real fear when I smell it," Mustache mutters. Reid is so grateful he doesn't know what to say.

"What are you doing way out here, kid?" That is the second man. Taller than his friend, leaner, with a nasty scar on one cheek that dimples the skin under his eye so he looks like he is constantly squinting. His blue eyes are hard and cold, and only skim over Reid as he speaks. The rest of the time he scans their surroundings. He reminds Reid of a gun-slinging hero from an old Western and he feels a surge of relief so big it takes his breath away for a moment.

"I don't know." Reid's words come tumbling out of him when he finally manages a breath, relieved they are there and real and are listening to him. "I was kidnapped and drugged and they dumped me here. There was a dead kid, I saw him and the hunters in black killed another kid, then the girl Monica and now they are chasing me!"

"Okay, you've got to slow down, boy." Mustache glances at Scar who nods once and starts a slow rotation of their position, gun held low but his finger near the trigger. He looks like it's a part of him. "What hunters? Like us?"

"No." Reid's hurried fear wishes Mustache would stop asking questions and take the threat more seriously. "We need to get out of here right now. Before they come back." Where are they? He knows they were right behind him. Why did they leave?

Maybe they are scared of the two men with the guns. Reid can only pray he is right.

"Let them," Scar says, voice a growl. "We've got lots of bullets. What are you thinking, Rich?"

Mustache just stares at Reid for a while, eyes narrowed to slits. "Not sure. Kid seems scared enough, might be telling the truth."

They don't have time to doubt him. Reid can't see the hunters, but he feels their eyes on him. And while it may just be his imagination playing tricks, he doesn't believe that's the case. "How did you get past the fence?" If they have a way out and Reid can find it, he will try to convince them to run with him. Or leave them there. At least they will have a fighting chance against the hunters.

Neither man says a word. They just exchange a look. Finally, Mustache says, "What fence?"

Reid resists the urge to shake him, not sure the man won't turn the gun on him. As much as this man could be his savior, the way he holds himself and his weapon is its own threat. "The giant electric fence," Reid says. "Back that way." He waves off in the distance, not quite sure he remembers where the fence is, but it doesn't matter. Both men shrug.

"Not sure what you mean, kid. We're just out for a bit of hunting. Looking for some game, a bit of shooting. You know. Sport."

How did they not see it? They must have encountered it at some point. Then, Scar laughs.

"Best game is usually kept locked up all neat and tight, right partner?"

Mustache grins and shrugs, eyes never leaving Reid. That is the answer he is looking for. They *do* have a way out. He intends to find it and use it with or without them. Hope flares up, fresh and powerful, and he finds himself grinning.

"Let's go!" He risks tugging at Mustache who jerks his arm away.

"Not so fast," the man says. "If what you're saying is true," and Reid can tell Mustache doesn't quite believe him, "we can't go just yet."

"Why?" They don't get it, don't understand how dangerous this is. And he has no way of impressing the danger on them without proof. The image of the gutted kid assaults him and he wishes they could see it, too.

"One," Mustache ticks off his index finger, "we're here to bag us some game. I didn't come all this way and fork out all that dough to walk away empty handed."

"Amen, brother," Scar says.

"And two," this time Mustache's middle finger goes down, "the worst thing you can do is let the enemy get behind you. Best to hit him face on and take him out before he can cause trouble. Am I right, bud-'o-mine?"

"As always," Scar says.

Reid doesn't know what to say. Or what to do when Mustache gestures with his gun for Reid to follow. He hesitates. He could risk it, run for the fence, hopefully find where they broke in. If they are that stubborn and downright stupid, he's not responsible for their safety.

He is about to run off when he hears it. The howl dissolves his hope, strips away his new found plan of escape and reduces him to a tearful child all over again.

When the last echo of it fades, Reid can barely breathe or stand. His knees quiver so much he is sure he will collapse at any moment. He won't survive another call, his heart will quit. He looks up and into Mustache's face. The man is very pale, brown eyes almost blotted out by his pupils, swollen by his own fear.

"What the hell was that?"

"I told you," Reid whispers. "The hunters."

Scar is next to them in an instant, voice low and deep, his urgency a cloud that envelops them all. "I've never heard anything like that before."

"Me either." Mustache chews on his namesake, eyes scanning the trees. "Damn it, we can't just leave."

Scar nods. "I'm not running."

Both men exchange a look before Mustache turns to Reid.

"Come on, kid," he says. "Let's go see what all the fuss is about." His words are confident, but Reid hears the quaver in them. Both men move forward in the gloom.

He can't go with them. It's the last place on earth he can go. His feet are lead, legs locked in place. Every nerve and fiber of his body begs him to run the other way. But he only heard one howl, one voice. For all Reid knows, they are surrounded. If he runs, leaves the men with the guns, he could be heading right into a trap. At least with them he has their weapons to protect him.

Swallowing a giant ball of fear, Reid stumbles forward and goes with them.

"Tell us about them." Scar stays close, eyes never resting anywhere for long.

"They're fast," Reid says, flinching from the memory of them. "They move like ghosts. I've never seen anything so fast."

"But they're men," Mustache says.

Reid's breathing tightens, his chest constricting. "They look like men."

Scar's hands adjust on his gun. "Well, we're ex special forces, kid," he says. "And nothing is faster than us."

Reid doesn't say anything. He can't. It won't do any good anyway. They are wrong. He watches them move and he knows in his heart the hunters are faster. But are they quicker than a bullet? Reid does his best to ignore the fact both men are criminals, illegal game poachers. He doesn't care. As long as they kill the hunters, they can shoot whatever the hell they want.

He considers asking them about rescuing the other kids and for the first time Reid actually lets himself wonder how many of them are out there and how many have already died at the hands of the black-dressed men. Lucy's beautiful face flashes in his head, but he forces her aside. When the hunters are killed, when Mustache and Scar show him the black-clad men can die just like anyone else, Reid will worry about the rest. But not until then.

Yet again he thinks about running for the fence. But by then they are deep into the forest, almost to the clearing. Reid feels a chill run up his spine. He holds back a little as the two camo-clad men move ahead of him, rifles ready. They go quietly, smooth movers themselves, rubber-soled boots barely making a sound on the littered path. Scar is the deadlier of the two in Reid's opinion, all sinew and cat-like grace. He feels his confidence rise. Maybe the men are right after all. They certainly look deadly to Reid.

Until he sees a flash of black in the trees and his heart stops beating. He can't breathe or call out and can only watch in horror as the three hunters drift around his salvation like spiders on a web.

Reid knows it is a trap before the men even notice the hunters are there. But again he is unable to act. Words freeze to the inside of his throat, his blood sluggish in his veins as his whole body sinks into shock.

Mustache finally spots the first hunter and spins, weapon ready, but too late. Reid doesn't even have the power to flinch as a shower of fine blood droplets arcs out from the man's throat. Mustache gurgles, weapon dropping to his side, suspended from the thick leather strap, swinging like a pendulum. Both of his gloved hands clutching at the arterial spray coating the nearby trees with red. Mustache half turns, knees buckling under him in a death dance, graceful as he falls. His eyes meet Reid's, more blood squirting out between his desperate fingers. The second blow is even faster than the first. Bile surges to Reid's throat when the hunter severs the man's head and sends it flying, spinning, spraying blood in a colorful arc. It lands at Reid's feet, sending more blood up and outward, the weight of the head rolling over to halt face up. Those brown eyes stare into his, the mustache dripping crimson into the dirt.

Scar has only a moment to shout, "Rich!" and raise his own rifle before his left leg is severed in one slice. His mouth gapes wide, the scar on his cheek pure white against his skin from the pressure of his fallen jaw as he looks down at his missing limb, nothing below his knee but air. The cut is so clean he is in perfect balance for a long moment, as though suspended by fine wire, a marionette gushing blood onto the ground. He topples in slow motion, gun swinging around. He fires one shot, another, but they go off into the forest, harmless. A hunter appears at his side, oozing close as he hits the dirt. Scar is rolled over onto his back in one smooth motion. The hunter's hand rises over the fallen man's abdomen.

Reid's sanity begs him to run, to get away and not watch, but he can't help himself or them. The first hunter bends over Mustache and together they slice downward, gutting both of the men in synch.

This is enough at last. Reid's feet are working again, his blood pumping. He turns and dashes into the forest, back on his original path, a new image there to replace the one of the dead boy.

Mustache gapes at Reid in his mind, the severed head his memory's new companion as he runs for his life.

9

This time when Reid runs, he sobs brokenly over the loss of his hope. He feels nothing for Mustache and Scar, not sure why his compassion has left him. He can only think of his own grief and, when the tears subside, the absence of the weapons the two men carried. Despite knowing the rifles were no help in the end, Reid still mourns leaving the guns behind. Not to mention the backpacks both men carried. The thought of what might have been in them is enough to drive Reid to distraction.

He can't afford distraction, not now. Who knows how long it will be before the hunters are on his trail again? And yet, he is starving and desperate and now knows just how deadly his pursuers are, able to take down trained soldiers, ex-military if Scar is to be believed. And Reid has no reason to doubt that is true.

He has to correct himself as he stumbles through the woods. Was. Was true. Scar won't be saying anything, true or otherwise, ever again.

In a moment of insanity, Reid finds himself giggling. Perhaps this is some funhouse, a joke, the gag on him. An elaborate carnival of terrors designed to bring the contestants to the brink, only to discover in the end it is a hoax. All the people he believes to be dead are really fine, hiding somewhere, laughing at him, in on it while he is desperately afraid.

The moment passes and the giggles dry up. Reid doesn't have time to create fictions around what is happening to him. He can't afford to slow down, to think in any way but for his own survival. This is no joke, not a hoax or a reality show gone wrong. It is real and his life is at risk.

He will die eventually. Reid has no doubt, especially now. How can he expect to survive when Mustache and Scar fell so easily, without even a fight, only two lonely gunshots to mark their passing? Reid has no illusions, not any more. But he'll be damned if they'll take him until the time comes he can't run any further.

He pulls himself to a halt at last, hoping the hunters stayed busy with the two men. That is enough to keep them occupied, it seems. They aren't following him, as far as he can tell.

It's all he has to cling to.

Reid catches his breath, shaking his head over and over as the image of Mustache's head tries to return and taunt him—the amazed look on his face, that this could possibly have happened to him, the staring eyes full of shock that he is dead. Accusing Reid of getting him killed in the first place. Reid looks down, sees the red stains on his jeans and sneakers. That and the replay of the arc of spraying blood is enough to twist his stomach into a fury of rejection.

Reid bends over, dry heaving, his insides trying their best to leave him, but only a little bile makes it to freedom. The tears start up again, a child's weeping, as he withdraws back into near infancy, the stress driving him to his knees. He hugs himself and rocks, bawling in waves of anguish, mucus from his nose dripping in long strings to pool in the dead leaves. His belly cramps again and he isn't sure if it is hunger or his body's last ditch effort to expel the rest of the terror inside him onto the forest floor.

Reid falls over, curling up on his side, unable to act. Small life goes on around him. Ants crawl past with bits of green waving above them. Hard-shelled black beetles trundle on their way, scuttling over the litter of twigs and pine needles. A fragile hummingbird hovers next to his face for a moment, examining him for a chance at some nectar before darting off when it realizes its mistake. He watches all this, letting the normal rhythm of the forest lull him out of his desperation and fear. Yes, he is still in as much danger as he was before. But the serenity of the world around him helps give him perspective.

Reid pulls himself together and sits up, looking around for shelter, mind back on survival. There, nearby. A clump of thick underbrush, heavy with leaves, enough to mask his presence. He crawls to it, his energy drained by his storm of emotion, the ability to drag himself along all he has left.

Reid parts the branches as best he can, to hide that he's disturbed the foliage, worming his way in as deeply as possible, before winding himself into the fetal position again.

He is suddenly cold, his whole body wracked in shudders, pins and needles of ice driving into his tender skin as his system reacts to his lack of food and water, taxed by the endless marathon he's been forced to endure. The outburst he released is simply the last straw placed on a pile of unsteady bricks he carries, enough to shove him over into physical reaction. Reid whimpers through it, teeth clattering together as the shivering gets worse. He recognizes he's in shock, but is unable to do anything about it.

Knowing it drives him back to desperation. This is the end for him and he is ready to admit it to himself. There is no way out. His despair won't even let him think about the two men and how they got over the fence. Because it no longer matters. He might as well try to reach the Moon as get to the fence at this point, let alone find their exit. Reid is going to die there and no one will save him.

He wallows for quite some time, long enough for the cold to slowly leave him and the shivering to stop. His weak and spent body feels heavy, listless. Moving is more effort than it is worth. Reid finds himself staring, without even the strength to care what his eyes are fixed on. He will stay like this forever, or until the hunters find him and kill him, whichever comes first. Reid doesn't care.

His body has other ideas. Clear of the shock that gripped him, his hunger resurges and slams him into the ground, bringing a rim of fresh tears to his eyes. He might not care if he lives or dies, but his body refuses to quit. Survival instinct takes over, his brain processing what it needs.

It refuses to stop until it gets those needs filled. It drives him to sit up, then to roll over onto his knees. He has to have food. *Has* to.

The animal in him hunts for something, anything to sustain him. His eyes fall on a lump of fur not far away. He scrambles on all fours toward it and looks closer.

It's a squirrel, dead and quiet. Reid ponders it for a long moment. Meat. It will sustain him. If he can find a rock… he won't eat the fur, but the flesh underneath should do the trick. Despite his ravenous cravings, he still hesitates. He has never killed anything before, beyond an ordinary spider or housefly. His father was no hunter, only an outdoorsman, and never taught Reid to kill. Fish, yes. Hunt, no. Although, his need reasons, he didn't kill this animal, nature did. But the thought of eating it is almost too much for his unsteady stomach to handle. Still, the primal part of him is so hungry he feels his mouth flood with saliva.

Reid finds a short stick and rolls the squirrel over. It's the first time he notices the small body is moving. His disappointment is sharp and quick and he considers killing it anyway. But wait. The movement is odd, rippling, and only in the animal's stomach.

Reid pokes the belly with his stick and the fragile, decaying skin erupts. A mass of fat, squirming maggots spill out over the dusty fur. Reid falls back with a cry of disgust, covering his nose with his T-shirt at the stench the open belly cavity releases. He has a flashback to the first dead boy, entrails bloated and shining in the moonlight and had he anything at all in his stomach, he would have thrown up again.

It takes him a while to recover. When he does, he looks around. Grass. Leaves. He knows they are edible, as long as he avoids certain ones. Poison oak and ivy, especially. As unappetizing as it may seem, at least it will give him something for his aching stomach to work over.

Reid pulls a handful of limp grass from the base of a tree and brings it with him to his hiding place. The stuff is thin and tough, but has some moisture in it. He knows from what his father told him it won't sustain him for long, but figures it's better than nothing. Reid doesn't dare risk mushrooms knowing most are poisonous, but he can start scouting for nuts and more grasses he knows he can eat. And if he can find another meadow, there is bound to be some dandelions or other edible plants to forage for. The idea actually perks him up and gives him some hope. He's precious low on anything resembling motivation, so he takes it as a good sign he's ready to move on.

Well, not quite. Reid lays in the undergrowth, pulling leaves from the bushes, taking advantage of the cover long enough to slowly fill his stomach. In the end, he simply stuffs them in his mouth, chewing and swallowing the precious morsels. But the greenery isn't what he craves, what his body really wants. The thought of meat won't leave him alone and he is unable to stop staring at the dead squirrel the entire time.

10

Reid must have dozed off, because he jerks awake in fresh terror at the howl of the hunters. They are far from him yet, but too close for any kind of comfort, if he had any to begin with. As he scrambles to his feet and checks his surroundings, he realizes the call itself is a weapon, designed to scare him and their other prey. Knowing it doesn't make it any less frightening, but the logical part of his mind that keeps trying to assert itself logs the information for later.

Reid also makes the connection between the hunters and wild animals. According to his dad, wolves cry out during the hunt as a method of herding their chosen meal into a trap. When Reid moves out, he understands that is probably the case with him as well. He hates to think their tactics are working, but doesn't have the courage or the heart left to do anything about it.

Until he remembers Monica and what she taught him. He's been running in straight lines, for all he knows heading right into their waiting arms. The image of her zigzagging her way through the forest triggers something inside him, a subtle but effective means of fighting back, even if only by staying out of the clutches of the hunters a little longer. He doesn't want to think about delaying the inevitable.

So, instead of heading directly away from the sound, he chooses a diagonal path. The trees are still sparse here, the undergrowth thin and simple to maneuver. The canopy is thick enough that most of the direct sunlight is blocked, making it easier to see.

Another howl pushes his pace forward. He considers taking his rebellion against their tactics one step further and resisting the urge to run, but knows he'll lose that fight. He reminds himself again that he needs to be smarter about it than he has been, less reacting and more planning. It's very hard to do without any real goals, suffering from a damaged and harried soul, but he keeps returning to the thought anyway.

He is rewarded by his evasion efforts when the next howl he hears echoes from a great distance. The diagonal path he is taking seems to be working. He sends a silent thank you to Monica, wherever her spirit is. Reid knows better than to get cocky, but he allows himself a brief arm-pump of victory before hurrying on.

After another long stretch of silence, he catches only the barest of sounds and knows he has finally managed to lose them. Either that or they decided to pursue other prey and let him live a while longer. He refuses to feel guilty this time. After all, he has no way of knowing if he's right. And even if he is, there is nothing he can do to stop it. He's done torturing himself over things he can't control.

Reid needs to remember what his goals are. Save himself. And save Lucy. Nothing else matters.

He slows then to conserve his energy, or what remains of it, and wonders how long he can keep this up. As he does, he catches a familiar scent and comes to an abrupt halt because of it. Wood smoke drifts on the still air. Reid spins in place, searching for the source. He moves on, sniffing as he does, trying not to compare his actions to that of the hunters.

There is the scent again, stronger this time. He is going the right way if he wants to investigate. And he very much wants to investigate. Reid can't see anything over or through the trees, but the smell is unmistakable. How many campfires did he sit at with his father, fires that smelled just the same? Reid tries not to think about those happy times. They won't help him now. Instead, he forces his weary legs into a jog.

The trees thin ahead, making it easier for him to spot the narrow meadow. He slows, nearing it with great caution. It must be a trap. That fact reasserts itself when he spots the weathered shack in the middle of the clearing, the grasses cut and pulled away as though someone purposely cleaned up. A trail of smoke puffs from the chimney, heading right for him.

Reid hunkers down on his haunches just inside the shelter of the trees and looks around, considering. It has to be a set up. There is no way anyone can survive the hunters. And yet, they themselves don't seem the type to use such a spot for a base. He considers this may have been where Mustache and Scar came from, but refuses to let go of the idea that they came over the fence. They had to have. And if this is where they were hunting from, it means the fence is near by. The other possibility is someone has survived and built this shelter as protection. Reid discards that idea immediately. No way. The hunters would tear this measly shack apart in a heartbeat.

It's much more likely whoever lives here or uses this place for shelter is in league with the hunters. Meaning, no friend of Reid's.

He waits a while longer, thinking if there is someone inside they have to move eventually. But no one does, at least, not that he can tell. And better yet, no one approaches. The sky in the west is turning red and orange and purple, but Reid is in no mood to enjoy the colorful sunset. He is grateful night is falling, plan already decided. Investigating the cabin is worth the risk. But only in full dark.

It is torture for him to sit there and simply wait and watch. He forces himself to patience, struggling back and forth between fear and focus, knowing he should keep running but needing to find out what is inside that shack. It becomes an obsession, as though freedom lies just beyond that door, some magic portal to a happier place. He'll regret it if he leaves without finding out, knowing he will think about it and let it distract him until he is able to see what's inside.

Leaving just isn't an option.

It's not until the sun is gone and he is surrounded by the dark that Reid realizes he has been on the run for a whole day. It feels like forever to him, a lifetime of fear and aching legs and worn out emotions. He's never been religious, neither were his parents, but Reid takes a moment and sends out an awkward prayer to the Universe for a way out and to say thank you for keeping his life.

He takes his time when he finally goes forward. Every step is calculated, every advance planned two moves ahead. He pauses often to listen, to look around him, especially when he makes it to the open. It's easier to move around without the pull of thick grass around his feet. Unchallenged, he reaches the rickety wooden door and peers cautiously through the uneven slats.

He's not sure what to expect, half of him thinking it might be empty and the other looking for Neverland. What he does see is so strikingly ordinary he feels some of his tension ease away.

Three cots line up against the far wall. The idea of a bed is extremely attractive. A bed of coals glows in the pot-bellied iron stove across from him, tucked into a corner. They cast just enough light to see by. Plenty. Reid can't believe it, but knows now more than ever he needs to find out what else is inside.

The door isn't locked. He eases in and pulls it shut most of the way behind him. Reid holds his breath, checking every corner in rapid succession, then the ceiling. Nothing. No one. He is alone.

The room is mostly bare, aside from the cots and three folding camp chairs arranged around the small stove. Sprawled next to the last one is a large, army-green duffle bag. Maybe his guess was right after all, and this was where Mustache and Scar were camping.

Reid crouches next to the bag and undoes the thick steel zipper. He draws a breath of shock and joy at the contents, never so happy to see ordinary objects before. He jerks free a pair of pants, a scratchy wool blanket. A large bottle of water winks at him in the glow of the coals. He digs deeper, finds matches, more water and, his stomach cramping in need at the sight, food. Power bars in crinkly metal foil, what looks like army rations and tins of beans and meat. Reid tears the wrapper from one of the bars and shoves the whole thing in his mouth, barely chewing before he swallows and stuffs in another.

He makes himself stop at two, not wanting to waste what he ate because of his gut's rebellion, remembering his first drink at the stream. For a long and horrible moment, as the food hits his belly, he is terrified that's exactly what is about to happen. But after a twinge of unease, his stomach settles and leaves him alone to do what he needs to do.

Reid discards his filthy jeans and pulls on the fresh pants, wishing he could manage a shower but feeling better for the clean clothes anyway. The khakis have a ton of pockets, which he fills with more food and a smaller water bottle. Finally, he's caught a break and he plans to take full advantage of it. The sight of all that stuff makes him greedy and he argues with himself over how much he can take. And run with.

He is just stripping off his shirt when a branch snaps outside, but in the distance. Reid freezes. Could be an animal. Could be the hunters. He isn't taking any chances.

The fresh T-shirt is on in a flash, his decision made without a thought. He takes the whole bag, the handles firmly grasped in his hand. He can discard what he doesn't use later, but for now he has to take it all with him.

Reid makes it to the door and peeks out. Movement. People, large people.

Hunters.

He panics and bolts, the bag dragging behind him. He is brought to an abrupt halt, sore right shoulder brutally jerked in its socket, when the duffel refuses to follow him. Reid allows a glance back. The heavy canvas is hooked on the door jam, one corner torn. He is out of time.

With a silent groan, Reid chooses escape over comfort. He releases his death-grip on the bag, letting the handles go with aching regret, and runs for the safety of the tree line. He pauses one more moment to look back as three shadows approach the shack. He sees them discover the bag, crouch over it, mutters growing louder as they communicate.

Time to go. Reid copies his earlier tactic and adds a new element. As he runs, he doubles back on his path, making it as hard as possible for them to follow him. The food in his stomach is just enough to give him energy to run until the moon rises.

Reid finds a thick bed of shrubs and squirms inside. There, he devours two more power bars and half the water. He snuffles the last of the crumbs from the packages, licking every last bit away, the sweet and salt stinging his tongue and making the insides of his cheeks tingle.

This time his stomach cramps for real. Reid lies down on the hard and uncomfortable ground, silently begging his body to hold on to what he has eaten. He breaks out into a cold sweat, waves of nausea beating against him, pain washing over his gut in cycles. He focuses on the moon hovering over the edge of the trees. How beautiful it is hanging there, shining down on him. His stomach clenches tight, punishing him for starving it for so long, before slowly easing and leaving him in peace.

Reid lies there for a while, letting the sweat dry in the beginning of the gentle breeze rising from the south. His hands explore his pockets and find only two more bars. The rest of his booty must have fallen out as he ran for his life.

Reid considers the cabin. He could stake it out, wait for another chance to raid it. Problem is, he knows they will be watching for him now. With deep regret, he lets it go and focuses on moving ahead. After all, he now has food and a bottle to hold water when he finds it. He's in much better shape than he was only an hour ago.

He had no idea his optimism had such resiliency and he finds himself grinning and wishing his father was there.

11

Reid finds himself settling into a half-run, half-lope he finds easier to sustain, like a workhorse so accustomed to his job he doesn't have to think about it anymore. It's so easy in fact, he feels like he is on autopilot, the ache in his legs and feet so familiar by now he hardly notices at all. And, in fact, would be thrown off rhythm if the pain went away.

The night slides by a determined step at a time. At one point he starts awake and realizes he has been dozing while running, his body taking over the necessary adjustments needed to make it through the thin underbrush. Not good. Not even remotely good. Anything could happen while he's in that state and he'd miss it, probably run right into it without knowing what he was doing. It frightens him enough to make him stop and take a break.

A new patch of underbrush in a new part of the forest, and yet it all feels the same to him. Reid devours another power bar, happy to have fuel, but so tired it doesn't really make much of a difference. He has to find a way to get his edge back, the sharpness that keeps him alert and ready to run for real. Nothing comes to him, no plan or way of forcing himself to focus. Coffee would be nice. Sleep in a real bed. After a shower. And a big, hot dinner. He jerks himself out of his daydream, so close to the real thing he wonders if he was actually sleeping this time.

Reid allows himself another five minutes before moving on.

When he steps out onto the path, swinging his arms and shaking his head in an effort to keep himself alert, he doesn't notice until he turns to move on that he isn't alone.

Reid freezes, face-to-face with a mountain lion. The reality of it is so absurd, he laughs.

All this time he has been terrified of the hunters and forgotten there must be natural predators in the forest as well. Bears, wolves, even giant and deadly cats like the one who glares at him are all as real a danger as anything else he faces. It's painfully obvious this is the case as his weary mind tries to decide what to do.

The cougar watches him, long tail twitching slowly back and forth, slitted eyes locked with his. The moonlight turns her coat into smooth silver, the ripple of muscle settling as she hunches forward, hindquarters tensed for the pounce. Reid's exhausted mind finds it ironic that it is likely he will now die from a big cat attack and wonders if the hunters will allow her to keep her kill if they find her with his body.

Her muscles settle, not even her tail in motion any longer. Her haunches drop this time as she falls very still. Reid finds her fascinating and stunningly beautiful crouched there in a pool of moonlight. He can't for the life of him muster any fear. She is amazing and majestic and falling to her will be a death he can accept.

A hunter howls in the near distance. The cat's attention snaps from Reid and turns toward the sound. Her huge ears swivel, catching the last of the echo while her whiskers ripple. She backs up a step, shaking her head, ears flattening as she hums a low growl in the back of her throat.

"You don't like them either, huh?" Reid is startled by the sound of his own voice. One of her ears twitches toward him but her focus, as intense as it was while she plotted him for dinner, is far away.

Her growl breaks off into a humming hiss. She disappears into the forest with one last flip of her tail. Reid stands there, hands shaking, but smiling after her. "Go get them, sweetheart."

He has to move. Wouldn't do to waste the gift she gave him and make himself such an easy target. Reid spins and starts out again. As soon as he does, he knows something is wrong with the ground. But he is too late to stop it when his foot slips. He falls, his arms flailing around him, trying to catch something, anything, to save him. His desperate grab only meets empty air. It seems to take forever before he lands on the ground below with a solid thud.

Reid gasps up at what he can see of the sky. At least the dirt under him is flat. Small consolation as he battles to draw air into his compressed lungs. A scattering of branches and leaves patters down on top of him, littering him with debris. He doesn't bother to swipe it away, instead studying the view above him while his body recovers. That can't be right. He can only see a small patch of stars.

He lies there for a while, getting his wind back, letting his body rest. As he does, he looks around, turning his head to the right and left. Dirt walls. More dirt walls. Debris he dragged down with him. A few branches, still heavy with leaves or needles. And him.

When he finally makes it to his feet, he approaches the sides of the hole. He feels the crumbling clay with his panic rising fresh to torment him.

The pit is man-made. The dirt is still reasonably damp, as though it was just dug. When Reid looks up again, he sees the crisscross net of woven branches that remain at the surface, a camouflaged covering. It explains the ones that lie scattered around him.

A trap, then. Maybe it was intended for the mountain lion. It could be the hunters liked all kinds of prey. But whatever the reason for it, Reid is in it and he has to get out. Now.

He digs his fingers into the soil and hoists himself up, the toes of his sneakers slipping across the moist earth. At first the going is very hard, the dirt so crumbly he can't get purchase. Before too long he is sweating and wrung out from the effort. But about half way up the fifteen or so feet he finds roots exposed and bits of rock, making the climb go much more quickly.

Panting, muscles vibrating from the effort to go faster, he is near the top and can see the edge of the moon. As he reaches for the lip of the hole, a hunter howls. It is so close it triggers his instinctual panic, sending his already taxes muscles into spasms. Reid throws all his weight onto his reaching hand and grasps the side of the gap, heart pounding his terror in his ears as he commits his escape to the fragile earth.

His hand grasps, grips. Holds his body up for a moment. And then it lets go, the thin, grassy roots within giving way with a terrible ripping sound, and he is falling again, out of control, tumbling back to the bottom.

This time Reid lies there for much longer, ready to quit. It's not fair and he can't do it anymore. He won't. Reid has done everything he possibly can to survive, done his absolute best. No one could ask more of him. No one.

When the next howl comes, it is almost on top of him, echoing down into the bottom of the hole, the taunting voice swirling around him on a playful wind. It drives Reid to his feet one last time. He may be lost, the hunters may get him, but he refuses to die in a pit, caught like a rat in a trap.

He digs in and tries again.

12

Reid draws a full breath and pulls himself upward. Every instinct he has prods him to go faster, climb harder, to claw and fight his way to the top, but he forces himself to take his time. It is the hardest thing he has ever done, but if he falls again, he is dead.

The hunters are near, but he has no way of knowing how near. The night air is deceptive, the mouth of the hole sending back echoes and lies. While his mind shrieks at him to hurry, he whispers back to it, *I have lots of time.*

He doesn't. They'll be on him in seconds. But it helps just enough to keep his pace steady, to still the shaking in his limbs so he can hang on and give him the boost he needs to reach the top of the hole again.

Time goes so slowly around him, pinching him between anxious fingers, squeezing the air from his chest and the fear out of his very pores. He longs to lunge for the top the same as the first time, but the sight of the missing patch of ground where it gave way under his weight is enough to hold him back. When he realizes his mistake, that in his fear he chose to climb the exact same section of wall instead of looking for a better route up, it almost defeats him.

Reid feels along the edge with his fingers, searching for purchase, something stable to hang onto. He finds only crumbling earth and thin grass. He continues to touch his way along the rim as far as he can reach, despair growing as he realizes there is nothing there to find. His toes burn from the strain of holding him up, his injured right shoulder, still a mass of bruises, threatening to let go and send him plummeting back to the bottom of the pit.

A small patter of dirt falls as his right hand slides over the root it holds. He has seconds to find a way out or he is done. The howl he dreads is so close now he is sure the hunter is watching him, waiting for him to fail, laughing at the pathetic weakness of his efforts.

Reid's hand starts to fall back and catches on something hard. He grasps at it, grips it tight. Tugs and burrows with his fingers. The root is old and gnarled, the remnant of a long dead tree. But it is solid and well anchored. This is the only chance he has.

With one last pull, the remainder of the strength in his right arm sacrificed to do it, Reid heaves himself up and over the edge of the hole. He feels himself starting to slide, the weakened side giving way under him. Reid desperately levers himself further forward, pulling on the ground to drag himself up, gouging out clumps of earth and grass to do it.

His toes finally catch on the surface and he forgets the ache in them instantly, driving his sneakers into the ground as hard as he can, instincts telling him to get away from the edge.

Reid is on his feet even as a hunter's howl drives a spike of terror further into his heart. There is a flicker on the path ahead. He is too late, no time to run.

The hunter has found him. But he's not trapped, at least. Not any more.

Reid sees the man in black flying toward him so swiftly he has no time to react. Or thinks he doesn't. The survivor in him takes over. He throws himself to the side as the hunter leaps, the image of an attacking cat. Reid's lungs empty of air in terrified exhalation, sure the blade of the man's knife is faster. He just registers the tug of the man's hands on his clothing as the hunter soars over him. Reid spins sideways and hits the ground hard on his right side, shoulder screaming at him, the pain so intense it slows him down. He tries to rise, his only hope that the man didn't notice the hole any more than Reid had.

Luck isn't with him. When he turns, he sees the hunter crouched on the edge of the pit, moonlight glistening on his teeth as he smiles at Reid. They look sharp, pointed like a shark's and very big. But it isn't the hunter's teeth he cares about. It's the strange knife in his hand, made of three blades all razor perfect and glittering silver.

Reid blinks. Wait. Not a knife, or knives. They are the man's hands. Claws extend from the ends of his fingers like sharpened eagle talons, the edges clearly honed to a deadly edge. Reid's brain rebels and he freezes, unable to comprehend what he is witnessing or believe it either. His logical mind refuses to accept, to put together the truth of what he is seeing, from the inhuman teeth to the claws for hands and, finally, the slitted pupils in solid silver eyes that fix him as firmly as the mountain lion's had.

While he struggles with reality, the hunter tenses and snarls at him, more animal than man in that instant, its intent clear. Reid knows if the thing—he can no longer think of it as human—had a tail it would be thrashing it at him. He can't help the comparison to the great cat this creature chased off with only the sound of its voice.

Reid has seconds, less than that, to live.

His luck, so far an absent friend, finally shows up to give him a fighting chance. As the hunter shifts its weight to pounce, the weakened lip of the pit suddenly gives way. Reid stares, mouth gaping open, wanting to run but sickly fascinated, as the black-clad thing struggles to recover and wonders in the rational part of his mind if he looked that silly when he fell.

The hunter is more dexterous than him and manages to regain one foot hold. Without thinking about it, Reid leaps forward and dives feet first, planting his sneakers in the center of the hunter's chest. It grabs for him, claws grazing his pant leg, tearing free one of the many pockets before it falls and lands with a loud thud.

This time Reid's horrible curiosity can't hold him. He doesn't stop to investigate or check if the thing is injured. He scrambles to his feet and runs. Reid can hear it howling behind him, from the bottom of the pit. Alive then, and sounding unhurt. Of course his luck wouldn't take him any further than that. He knows the hunter won't be long getting out. But fate has given Reid a head start and he has no intention of wasting it.

He runs on.

13

The night passes him by. When the sky ahead of Reid lightens yet again, he is surprised to find he is still alive. Surprised, and very grateful. He has no idea why the hunter didn't catch up to him in the dark, but he'll take the time he's been given.

In the meantime, he struggles with accepting what he saw. His logical mind and his emotions fight for control, arguing constantly between what is real and what can't possibly be true. But he knows what he witnessed, can see the creature's hands, the pointed teeth, the eerie eyes. All of that added to the way the thing moved and Reid finds it hard to deny.

Whatever the hunters are, they can't be human. At least, not completely. If they ever were in the first place.

But none of it makes sense. Are they an experiment gone wrong? Some mad scientist's private army of soldiers bent on world domination? It seems so ridiculous he rolls his eyes at himself. This isn't some bad TV show, or a B movie at two a.m. on a Sunday morning. Besides, he's pretty sure there's more to it than anything he could ever imagine.

Not that what he thinks matters, considering the circumstances. He's done deceiving himself, though, through lying in the face of perceived reality. This enclosure, the fence, the kidnapping, all of it leads to one thing and one thing only. He and the other kids he's encountered are nothing more than target practice.

Reid knows it's irrelevant who is responsible, but he longs to find out, just so he has someone to blame. It's too hard to pin it on the hunters because he is so afraid of them. Mustering anger toward them is just too hard to sustain. He waffles back and forth between Lucy and her boss, Mr. Syracuse, but it's really difficult to stay mad at his sister when he knows she is as much a victim as he is, and in as much trouble, if not more. He has no face to give her mysterious benefactor, so his imagination musters a cartoon-like character too ridiculous to focus his rage on either.

Reid rolls all of this around in his head as the morning light briefly cheers him. Only then does he notice the terrain has changed. His calves have ached for so long he didn't notice the incline until he is able to see it. The ground is rocky as well, more like the edge of the ravine where he left the fence the night before last. Reid turns and looks back the way he came, worried he has somehow gotten spun around but corrects himself. Since he turned from the electric barrier, he has been moving east all along. Unless whoever dumped him here also managed to change the path of the sun.

Honestly, if someone told him at that moment he wasn't even on Earth anymore, he wouldn't question it. Everything around him is just too surreal.

There is a small break in the trees ahead and he peeks out to have a look before risking exposing himself, wondering if he survives this will he ever feel completely safe in the open ever again. He doubts it very much.

When Reid finally sees where he is going, his breath catches.

Ahead is a low peak, covered in soft wood trees, but almost mountainous, rolling away into the distance. To his right runs a valley with a river running through it, looking like a sliver of blue and sliver, sparkling at him, instantly triggering his thirst. To the left are more trees and the continued incline.

Reid steps back into the shadow of a clump of spruce and does some thinking. So much for some alien planet. This just looks too much like a place he's been before. He's known since the first night he can't be in his native Arizona any longer, not with the forest he's been running through. But the scene ahead looks achingly familiar and he doesn't want to believe it. It can't be possible he's this far from home. Just the idea of it makes this immeasurably worse even though he can't explain to himself why.

His father took him camping in New Hampshire once when he was ten. It looked the same as his surroundings now. His mind flashes to cool nights, a well-kept campfire, his father smiling at him. Flames reflected in his sea-green eyes the exact shade of Reid's and on his dark hair Reid also inherited. His father used to joke they were peas in a pod and Reid loved that. Especially when they camped in the forest, only a sleeping bag and what they could carry to sustain them. His father never believed in tents, instead insisting Reid learn how to make his own shelter.

He's very grateful, even though he hasn't had much of a chance to take advantage of all those old lessons. He's been too busy running.

The trouble is, if the surroundings are the ones Reid recognizes, that means he is thousands of miles from home.

He finally realizes why it bothers him so much. Reid holds all of his memories of his dead father dear to him and having this place, the same kind of place, taking over his treasured time with his dad does strange and terrible things to his already aching heart.

He could be wrong. There are forests everywhere. Oregon, for example. California. Equally as far and remote. Alaska? Or Canada even. But he knows in his bones he is right. Reid shudders. The compound is somewhere in the North Eastern US. It's June. That makes sense. It is warm enough during the day and not too cold at night although he hasn't really stopped moving so he sort of ignored the temperature so far. But the longer he is here, the worse conditions could get. He may be forced to hide during the day if the temperatures get too hot.

He's been lucky so far when it comes to insects, and wonders where the black flies and mosquitoes are, constant companions the last time he stayed overnight in the woods. Not that he's complaining or anything. Being a snack for ravenous bloodsuckers while running from the hunters would just add another level of hell to his situation. But it also reminds him just how controlled this whole thing feels.

Reid glances up at the clear blue sky and wonders how long the weather could hold. Rain would also make his life more miserable than it already is, although he takes it as a good sign he is even thinking about his surroundings and not totally focused on just putting one foot in front of the other.

He considers the food he has left, wondering if he should ration it further before shrugging to himself. Now or later, he needs the energy. He polishes off the last power bar and the final swish from the water bottle. The wrapper he hides under a rock, but the empty plastic container he tucks into one of his pockets. The river he spotted below is probably fed by the stream he encountered, and that means fresh water. He will need a container to store some in just in case the hunters chased him off for the second time. His thirst demands he find a way to never go without again.

Reid moves on, keeping to the east, which means climbing. He is relieved he hasn't heard any hunter's howls for a while and wonders if they ever sleep. He's not exactly feeling safe, but as the climb gets harder he admits he is dead on his feet and needs to find somewhere to rest. It's either that or pass out where he stands and make himself a ripe target.

Easier said than done. Reid starts looking, not for pursuers but a hidey-hole he can use, even for a few hours of rest. Tucking into the shrubbery worked fine in the dark, but in daylight he's not so sure. Besides, the undergrowth has thinned and he's having a hard time finding a place that would conceal all of him.

Reid considers a tall tree, the lower branches just within his reach, but quickly discards the idea. He would have to climb too high to be safe and out of notice, so high that if he fell he would definitely be hurt. He doesn't have rope or anything else to tie himself to the tree, so climbing is out. The idea of breaking a leg or suffering a concussion is enough to drive him onward.

As for building his own shelter, Reid decides to leave that as a last resort. It would take a great deal of time and precious energy to gather the materials he needs. Even then he isn't sure he would feel comfortable trusting something he built. Had his father been with him, with his mad survival skills handed down from his father… but Reid is on his own.

He continues for another few minutes, sneakers sliding over brown spruce needles and damp moss before he spots what looks like a gap in the rock face ahead. He is fairly high by now, the cliff he stands on allowing him a better view of the world below. He pauses, panting, and has a good look around, so self conscious about exposing himself he tucks behind a tree and only pokes out his face.

Everything is very green in the new light of day, softly hazy to the west where a thin line of fog hugs the edge of the valley. A strip of gray winds its way in the distance, sparkling objects speeding by. The interstate. He tears his eyes from it. There's no hope there, he knows it, but at least he's found that edge of the fence again, giving him some perspective on how far he's come. He's actually amazed by the distance he has covered and how high he has climbed.

The scene is so peaceful and surreal, Reid wants to scream. Under the thin veneer of evergreens there is nothing peaceful about it. And yet, to an objective observer, it is the picture of calm and serenity. Trees stretch out far below him and, in the distance, he is sure he sees the edge of the fence catching the light. Other than the odd bird drifting from canopy to canopy, nothing else moves.

Reid turns and approaches the gap. This close he realizes it's not just a crack in the rocks, but an opening to something more. He hoped for the tiny shelter the rocks he envisioned would provide. The idea of a full-blown cave stirs his excitement.

A sliver of fear surfaces. If he goes in, if he chooses to rest there, he might be trapped. Panic raises his blood pressure, pounds his heart. He glances around, suddenly sure the hunters lie in wait for just such an opportunity to trap a stupid kid. But he is as alone as before and so desperately tired he considers the cave mouth again.

Maybe there is a second exit. If so, he would consider it. Trouble is, there is only one way to find out. He has to go in.

Reid steps up to the entrance, noticing a small pile of broken branches draped over part of it. He hesitates. It looks like a trap all right. Those breaks are deliberate, not an accident or caused by the weather, and the pile is artful, as though carefully arranged. So it can't be the hunters. They are too careful, too meticulous. Which means kids, maybe. Like him. Could it be someone sheltered here before him? Or even, was it possible, could still be here?

Reid rolls his shoulders forward as he shrugs to himself. If the cave is empty, but useful, he's in luck. And if there are others, well… maybe they have answers he doesn't. Either way, it's worth the risk, no matter his fears.

Reid draws a steadying breath and ducks inside.

14

"Don't come any further."

It's a girl's voice, quavering and low. Reid can feel the fear radiating toward him, almost smell it in the cool and damp of the cave. It is so dark inside, his eyes still tuned to the sunny morning, he is forced to wait out the adjustment, all the while hating how vulnerable it makes him and refusing to back off at the same time.

There is a whisper of cloth, the sound of a shoe grinding over dirt and rock. A thin channel of light penetrates the darkness and someone glides into it. Not a girl, so she isn't alone. This boy is small, scrawny even, his skin so dark he almost blends into the gloom around him. Reid guesses he's about thirteen or so. His vision slowly adapts, enough he spots two more figures hiding in the cave.

"I'm Reid." He figures it's the best place to start. The least threatening. But the boy before him doesn't look all that reassured. He has the same tension in him Reid saw in Monica, though less desperate and more sane.

"What do you want?" The kid's voice shakes. Reid knows the feeling well.

"Nothing." That much is true. Not from him or his friends. "I just saw the cave and thought I'd check it out."

He whispers, his voice drifting in the dark. Reid isn't sure he'll ever speak above a whisper again. Just in case.

"Milo." The boy says, grudging and with a scowl on his face. "This is our cave."

Reid shrugs like he doesn't care, even though it hurts him, this rejection from his own kind. "Nice of you to share." He can't help that parting shot and a part of him hopes it cuts deep.

He eases backward, ready to leave, when the girl comes into the thread of light. "It's all right," she whispers back. "You can come in. If you want."

Reid hesitates. He does want to, very much. Just seeing the three of them together in that sheltered place gives him a feeling of safety. He knows it isn't smart to let that feeling in, but he can't help himself. He's been running for so long.

Still, Milo's initial rejection makes Reid pause. Pride reaches out and slaps him so hard he flinches.

"I know when I'm not welcome."

He holds his place anyway, waiting for one more encouraging word.

Relief floods him when the girl obliges. "Please," she says, gesturing with one hand. "We need to stick together."

At last, someone understands. Reid thinks of Monica. If only he had gotten to her before her mind snapped and fear took her over. He slides into the cave and out of the path of the light, allowing the cool darkness to wrap around him. The scent of the earth is stronger here, and unwashed bodies. But he doesn't mind, pretty sure he's just as fragrant.

The girl leaves the light, Milo right beside her. She shines even in the dark, pale blonde hair almost glowing. "I'm Leila."

Reid lets his legs buckle and slides to the floor, wrapping his arms around his knees.

"This is Drew." She introduces a second boy. There is a subtle flash, the hint of light on glass as the kid nods once.

"Wish I could say it's nice to meet you." Drew's voice is almost as high as Milo's, but with an odd accent. Reid's mind says New England. So this kid is local.

Leila makes the first move, easing forward until she is face-to-face with Reid. She is about his age, her eyes as light as her hair, dark bruises underneath highlighting them. Even her skin is ghostly pale, thick eyelashes transparent. Reid almost laughs when his heart tells him she is beautiful.

Not the kind of thing he needs to be thinking about at a time like this.

"How long?" She sits next to him.

"This is my second sunrise," he says.

Drew and Milo join them, Leila's bravery obviously setting them free of their wariness.

"I'm on day three," Milo says. His white teeth flash against his dark skin when he speaks.

"Me too," says Drew. Glasses, braces, chubby cheeks. Pushing fourteen if Reid could guess. Drew hitches up his pants as he sits. They bag around his still-thick waist.

"I'm two days in." Leila smiles at the boys. "They found me right away. I'm pretty lucky."

Reid agrees. A jagged stab of jealousy takes his breath away for a moment.

"Drew found me," Milo says. "Not like being together helps all that much."

Drew is nodding, glasses hiding his eyes, the dark turning them into oval mirrors.

"If I ever get out of here," he says, "I'm never running another step ever again."

The other two laugh. Reid can't bring himself to.

"How long have you been hiding here?" It would be nice to think the cave could be a more permanent refuge, but Leila sighs.

"Since early this morning, just before dawn. They seem to find us no matter where we go."

Reid fights off the instinctual panic. "Is there another way out of here?"

None of them say a word. It's answer enough.

"We tried to hide the entrance," Drew says. "Didn't do a good enough job, obviously."

"Do you have any food?" Milo sounds pathetic and Reid instantly recoils from the boy's need. He knows then, even if he had any left, he would lie and wonders what he is becoming.

"No," Reid says. Then, reluctantly, he tells them about the cabin and what he found.

They listen to him like he is a prophet, locked onto his words.

"We should go right now!" Drew is on his feet, hands

tugging at his falling jeans. "I bet we could sneak in and out and they'd never know."

Reid reaches out and pulls the boy back down to the ground. "They know I was there," he says. "They'll be watching now."

"But we're starving." Reid despises the whine in Drew's voice and resists the urge to slap it out of him. He reminds Reid of Lucy and how she used to beg their parents for the things she wanted. It makes him sick to his stomach.

"There are things in the forest we can eat." He has been so focused on running he forgot that was true. But his father showed him what to look for. The right kinds of mushrooms. Fiddleheads. Bird nests could hold eggs. He just needed enough time to look.

Reid realizes he is still thinking in singular terms, sad he is obviously ready to abandon the others at the first sign of trouble.

"Do any of you know why we're here?" More than food or water or shelter, Reid wants answers. But the three shake their heads all at once.

"We've asked ourselves the same questions." Leila's eyes drift toward the light coming through the entrance of the cave.

They are so pale they are transparent in the glow of the sun. "But we all have the same story. I was taken from my bed in the middle of the night by a group of men who drugged me. I woke up in the back of a van, was carried out here and dumped in the dark." Her thin shoulders rise and fall once. "The boys found me, got me loose. Told me we had to run." She turns back, eyes meeting Reid's. "Do you have anything new to add?"

He shakes his head. "Sounds about right." Reid sighs, his weariness settling around him like a blanket. If he doesn't get up and start moving soon he knows he will pass out. "Are you foster kids too?"

All three nod. "We figure we're easy targets." The bitterness in Drew's voice is nothing new to Reid. "No one will miss us, you know? The system will call us runaways so no one comes looking or gives a crap."

"Have you seen anyone else?"

"Just other kids," Milo says. "And not for long." By the way he says it Reid figures those kids didn't make it.

"Have you gotten a good look at the hunters?"

Milo's shudder is so violent he has to hug himself. But it's Drew that speaks.

"Why?" The boy trembles, hands rubbing across his thighs over and over.

"Just wondering." Reid isn't sure he wants to voice what he is thinking. He cares enough about the possibility of staying with them at this point he doesn't want them to think he is crazy. But Drew won't let it go. He reaches forward, chubby fingers tapping Reid's sneaker. He pulls back before Reid can react, a frightened animal looking for attention.

"Why?" Drew repeats the question. Reid can't tear his eyes away from his reflection in the boy's glasses.

"Because," he finds himself saying, "I don't think they are human."

No one says anything for a moment and in that time Reid berates himself for making a terrible mistake. He may have been willing to abandon them for his own safety at first, but the past few minutes have made it harder and harder to consider running by himself again.

"I knew it!" Drew reaches over and punches Milo in the arm. The smaller boy rubs the sore spot and scowls at his grinning friend.

"You did?" Relief is welcome. They won't shun him after all. Although the look on Leila's face is suddenly so lost and grief-stricken Reid wishes he hadn't spoken at all.

"There's no way they are human." Drew shoves his glasses back with one finger, head bobbing in his excitement. "They move too fast. Those claws they've got! Their eyes…" he shudders. "And that howl. Like an animal."

Reid finds himself nodding. "Then what the hell are they?"

"Alien invasion." Milo groans at that and even Leila rolls her eyes and offers a ghost of a smile. But Drew is adamant. "What else could they be?"

Reid is as skeptical as the others, but doesn't have an answer.

"Dude, you watch too many movies." Milo doesn't sound convinced.

"I'm telling you," Drew goes on, his excitement obvious, "it's got to be an invasion. Some kind of foothold situation."

"Then why the fence?" Reid gets the impression this is an old argument because Leila has looked away from them, lost in her thoughts. At the word *fence* she swivels her attention back to him.

"What fence?" Milo is the first one to ask, his voice squeaking out at the end of the word.

"Big, metal, deathly electric." Reid looks from face to face. They obviously have no idea what he is talking about. "I was following it for a while, but had to stop."

They are all quiet for a bit as they process this.

Reid gives them a little time before telling them about the two men and how easily the hunters took them down, weapons or no weapons. They are visibly shaken.

"It's hopeless, then." Milo shudders out a sob. "No one can save us."

"We already knew that." Drew tries for tough but Reid sees right through him, hearing the tears the boy chokes off. "We're on our own out here."

Leila is silent, eyes on the ground, her whole body still. "How did they get in?"

Reid is impressed with her. "The fence."

Drew's glasses flash as he turns his head to refocus on Reid. "There's no way," he says. "If it's electric, like you say, it would have killed them getting over."

"Somehow they did it," Reid snaps back. Drew shrinks from him and Reid instantly feels guilty. "I don't know how," he says, gentler this time and Drew relaxes. "But I mean to find out."

"Do you really think we can get out?" There is no hope in Leila's voice. Only the same calm and quiet she has shown him all along.

Reid doesn't answer her.

"Why would someone fence us in?" Leila looks so tormented by this new information Reid wishes he kept this information to himself.

"Maybe they are specimens," Drew says, still clinging to his alien theory. "Being tested or something."

"More like we are," Reid mutters.

"That's the lamest ass thing I've ever heard." Milo turns away from Drew. Lost to his usual audience, the chubby boy turns his attention to Reid.

"What do you think?"

It's a moment before Reid answers. In the meantime Leila and Milo focus on him. Reid thinks about it, considers what Drew said before shrugging his shoulders forward when the truth of the whole thing rolls through him.

"I think it doesn't matter all that much," he says, finally admitting it to himself. Answers aren't what he needs. He doesn't care anymore. Reid just wants to get away.

The others are silent. Reid shifts positions at last, breaking the quiet, his head aching and body unable to rise.

"So what now?" He hadn't meant to ask them, the question more aimed at himself than the others, but Drew speaks up.

"We don't know." He exchanges glances with first Milo, then Leila. "The fence thing sounds good."

Reid slumps sideways, his eyes so heavy he can barely focus. "Yeah," he says, stumbling over his words, "it does."

A cool hand touches his cheek, long hair tickling his ear as Leila bends over him.

"Get some rest," she whispers. "We'll watch over you until it gets dark. Then we'll decide what to do."

He fights the exhaustion, still not trusting completely, but his body doesn't give him a choice. Reid is dragged under and into sleep.

He surfaces briefly, twice. The first time he jerks awake from a horrible dream he can't recall and falls right back into unconsciousness. The second time he wakes to heated whispers, but even that can't keep him up for long.

When he wakes the third time, he instantly notices the utter quiet. Reid sits up, bones and muscles crying out in protest, but he ignores them as he looks quickly around.

He is alone. His heart clenches, stomach a solid knot of rage. They left him, abandoned him there after they promised they would watch over him. She *promised.*

So much for trust.

A howl echoes nearby. Reid freezes, his anger running out of him, shoved aside by terror. A flicker makes it through, the thought that they set him up to save themselves, but he has no time to let it trouble him. Fear shoves him toward the gap and out into the night. He has slept the day away, his only consolation. And yet, if that rest gets him killed, it will have done him little good.

Reid eases down the hill toward the thicker trees, all senses wide open and alert. He waits for another call to reach him, but none comes. Reid finds the head of a path into the trees and runs for it.

He slams right into Leila. She falls back but he catches her, holds her up until she has her balance again. She looks up into his eyes, hers full of the terror they share.

"Hurry!" Her whisper is a hissed command. She turns without another word and runs down the trail. Reid follows right on her footsteps, keeping up with her easily. She leads him on a winding run through the trees, dodging the path over and over. He realizes she too understands the value of avoiding straight lines.

She stops once, alert and frightened. Reid waits with her, heart in his throat, as a shuffling black shape snorts its way through the forest. Panic gives way to more ordinary fear as the black bear fixes them with its shining dark eyes. Rather than attacking, it growls gently before plodding off into the dark.

Leila rests against a tree, her breath easing out of her. When her eyes meet his, she smiles. "If this wasn't so horrible, that would have been amazing."

He finds himself smiling back. "I'm sorry." The words blurt out of him. "I thought you left me behind."

She is quiet for a long time before shrugging her shoulders once. "We did," she says. "But I had to come back for you."

Reid's blood, once warmed by her friendship, runs cold again. "Why is that?"

"Who knows," she says, moving off, "maybe we need you after all." She stops, turns, looks at him. "Are you coming?"

He wants to say no. They betrayed him, left him to die. Why should he? But he can't bring himself to be alone again. Instead, he follows her into the forest while he builds walls around his budding trust and compassion.

15

It isn't long before they catch up with Drew and Milo. Both boys look guilty, refusing to meet Reid's eyes. He ignores them, turning instead to the two other kids huddled nearby.

"This is Carly and Trey." The girl Carly is so skinny it hurts Reid to look at her, her gigantic dark eyes pleading for someone, anyone, to save her. Stringy hair sways around her as she shivers in the cool of the night. The boy Trey's skin is lighter than Milo's, his body taller. He has a constant twitch in one cheek. Reid wonders if it's new since he was dumped here.

"We have to go." Leila glances over her shoulder. She doesn't have to say it twice.

Reid takes the lead without thinking about it, so accustomed to being alone he barely considers what the pecking order might be in the little group. But when he glances back at them no one complains. In fact, if anything, they look relieved.

Which makes him uncomfortable. He's no leader and tells himself he'd better speak up about it the next time they stop for a rest.

Reid heads off at an angle toward his best guess. His eastward path is leading him away from the fence and he needs to get back to it. He hates to recover old ground, but has little choice. All of his private hope rests on finding where the two men came through. He doesn't allow himself anything else.

Reid does his best to head west, but about an hour or so into their stumbling jog he checks the moon. For the first time his sense of direction seems to have deserted him somewhat. He can tell he's off course, heading more south, and swears at himself a little. Then shrugs. He can only imagine they are surrounded by fence. Not like it matters how they get to it as long as they do.

Reid checks on the kids behind him. He is surprised he is alone. Have they abandoned him again? He fights down a surge of fury as he spots Trey emerging through the trees. Carly stumbles along with him, hunched over almost in half. Leila struggles beside the girl, one hand on her elbow, the other on her back. When they join Reid, Leila's pale eyes lift to his. Her anger sends him back a step.

"Thanks for waiting." Leila looks away, returning her attention to the skinny girl next to her. Carly gasps for air, mewing whimpers filled with despair cutting Reid to the bone. He shoves remorse aside as Milo half-jogs, half-drags himself to a halt next to Trey.

"Where's Drew?" Reid is troubled and more than a little guilty. He should be more careful. He didn't even think to check if they were keeping up. The survivor in him is disgusted and wants to abandon them, as weak as they are. He shoves that aside, too. Like it or not, he chose to run with them and he won't change his mind unless they give him a good reason.

"Here." Drew drops out of the dark, collapsing at Reid's feet, his glasses fogged from perspiration. The boy's face is flushed and slick with sweat, obvious even in the dark.

Reid silently examines himself and is pleased to discover that aside from hunger and thirst, he is feeling okay. Strong even. The food he found is sustaining him. For now.

"We need a break." Leila helps Carly sit down. Reid's urgency tugs at him while the rest try to catch their breath.

"I'll scout ahead." He leaves them there before anyone can protest and moves on. He can't bring himself to sit still, not after two days of running and with the possibility of freedom so close.

The trees thin ahead, so he slows his pace. The moon is high by then, the still cloudless sky full of sparkling stars. Reid feels a grin break over his face as he looks out across the small, glittering lake below. There is a brief but steep decline to reach it but he knows he can handle it without a problem.

His thirst is so strong he almost moves on without the others. With a groan of denial, he turns and goes to get them.

"Water," he says when he reaches them, still sprawled on the ground. He doesn't have to say anything else. They are up and moving immediately.

It's not long before they stand on the lip of the cliff looking down. Drew makes a soft sound and shuffles his feet, sending a slide of small rocks down the decline.

"I can't." His fingers shove his glasses back on his face with such fierceness Reid is startled.

"We'll help you," Leila says.

But Drew shakes his head and backs away. "Heights," he says. "I just can't."

Reid doesn't think, only trusts his instincts. He bypasses the others, seizing Drew and throwing him over his shoulder.

A brief shriek escapes the boy, quickly silenced, but the sound carries into the forest.

Reid slides down the steep slope and is on the bottom within seconds. He sets Drew down on his own two feet and looks up at the others.

"I don't want to hear *can't*," he says.

The rest of the kids descend more slowly, but make it safely to the bottom. Reid leads them to the water, studying the surroundings carefully. Like the stream, he knows this could be a perfect trap opportunity for the hunters, but the call of the lake is too strong to resist.

Reid waits for the others to drink, instinctively watching over them. A fierce surge of protectiveness races through him even while he wars with his mind. He is faster than them, stronger. It would be easier to simply leave them here and go on alone. They are pathetic and weak. But they are human like him, kids like him and being with them helps remind him of his humanity.

When Milo steps back, Reid falls to his knees and plunges his face into the cold water. It is as icy as the stream but calm and, remembering his first experience, he takes his time.

He requires a great number of mouthfuls to slake his thirst, but when he is done, Reid takes another moment to rinse and fill the bottle, tucking it away into the side pocket of his stolen pants. He is about to rise when he hears a cry and a splash, and jerks around to look.

Someone is in the water, thrashing around. Reid runs to the spot and finds Milo gesturing at Drew.

"Swim back!" Milo makes unhelpful motions with his hands, like it does any good. Drew goes under before glugging his way back to the surface. His glasses and braces shine in the moonlight, but he remains silent in his distress.

"What happened?" Reid freezes with indecision.

"It's deeper than it looks." Leila is there next to him, panic in her face. "Drew, swim!"

"He fell in." Milo is crying. "It's my fault. I wanted to know how deep it was."

Trey and Carly huddle together and refuse to look, faces buried in each other's shoulders.

Drew goes down again. Reid knows he needs to let the boy drown. He can't risk getting sick or hypothermic in a rescue attempt. The water is just too cold. But he is already shedding his sneakers and socks, handing the water bottle to Leila. He dives in before his logical thoughts can stop him.

The shock of the water temperature is almost enough to drive him under. Reid gasps at the cold, but forces himself to stroke forward, reaching Drew with little effort. The boy latches onto him instantly, his panic making him a horrible weight with tearing hands and thrashing feet. Reid fights to calm the boy, but knows sound travels over water and can't risk talking him down.

It is a grim and silent battle, one that quickly wears Reid out. He has gone under so many times because of Drew's fear, he knows one more will be the end of them both. Reid does the only thing he can do. He puts both hands on the boy's shoulders and shoves him under the water, holding him there.

Drew battles as hard as he can but soon weakens, his panicked energy almost run out. Reid waits two more heartbeats before letting the boy rise to the surface. Drew does, choking out water, eyes huge behind glasses he's managed to hang onto through it all.

"You have to stop fighting me." Reid risks that whisper. "Drew, stop."

Drew chokes on some more water. His teeth chatter together and Reid knows his own are close behind. His legs are numb from the cold, hands on fire in it. They don't have much time left.

Drew nods at last, clinging but not struggling any longer. Reid turns, his weariness making him slow, and searches for the shore. He groans very softly as he realizes the edge is no longer reachable.

In the course of their struggle, they have drifted far from the others. Reid turns them around, paddling gently to avoid more sound and conserve his strength. All around them is only more water. Until he turns west. There is the opposite bank, still far but the closest of any. Reid draws a breath and strikes out.

The water is heavy on his limbs, Drew's weight pulling him down. He feels the boy's legs moving and knows he is trying to help but has to stop. It's throwing Reid off kilter. "Don't do that," he whispers. Drew's arms tighten around his neck.

"Sorry."

Reid reaches out again, legs kicking in slow rhythm. He has always been a good swimmer, a strong athlete, but the cold is seeping his strength from his body and he knows they won't make it. Like that matters. He still has to try.

Swimming becomes as automatic as running had, Reid's mind drifting as he puts one arm in front of the other, over and over again. The shore is drawing nearer, but his vision blurs so he can't tell how much closer. He can't feel his body anymore, not even sure he is still swimming. Water slaps his face, goes in his mouth and he splutters and coughs on it. He can hear Drew breathing in his ear when he turns his head and the slosh of the waves he makes.

Reid is done. His arms won't move any longer. His legs give out at the same time. He forgets why he was fighting so hard and lets himself slide under the water.

Something tugs at him, pulling him forward. Whispered voices say his name, his numb skin barely feeling it when his clothes are pulled free. His skin starts to return to life and he cries out, low and painful, the ache of warmth making him writhe in agony. When he finally registers contact, he almost pulls away from what holds him. It's like he's been plunged into fire. For a long time he simply whimpers and shivers, lying there, ready to die.

He is surprised when he opens his eyes at last and finds Leila looking down at him. She is holding him to her and they are draped with bits and pieces of clothing. He spots Milo and Drew in the same position while Carly and Trey huddle nearby, shivering in the night air, their jeans and sweaters the source of warmth that kept Reid alive.

"Drew," he whispers.

"Fine," Leila says. "You got the worst of it because you were swimming."

He doesn't have the strength to nod. "Didn't think we'd make it."

She hugs him. His tender skin protests, but he doesn't tell her to stop.

"Me either," she says. "That was amazing."

Reid closes his eyes again. When he opens them, Drew is there. His glasses are missing and for the first time Reid sees his eyes. They are silvery in the moonlight.

"Thank you," the boy says. "You saved my life."

Reid thinks of a snappy comeback, but it's not worth the effort. "You're welcome."

"Reid…" Drew looks away, puts his glasses back on. Looks back. "I was the one who wanted to leave you behind."

Reid just nods. Drew hugs him, the impulsive move making Reid groan from the pressure of it.

"We need to go soon." Carly's voice carries. Reid struggles to sit up and manages. He is still cold, but his body is all present and accounted for and he is very grateful.

Reid is about to ask why she is so afraid when he hears it. A howl. Very close. It's enough to get him up and pulling on his wet clothing. Leila hands him his socks and sneakers, fortunately dry. He isn't sure how far he can run in his condition, but knows he doesn't have a choice.

He has just finished tying his shoelaces when Carly's scream jerks him upright. He looks where she points and freezes, cold again, this time from fear.

Two hunters hover on the other shore of the lake. They hold still for only a moment, the girl's scream carrying across the water to them, before beginning a lazy lope around the bank.

Reid grabs Carly and drags her along, forcing his exhausted body to move, pulling the terrified girl with him, following the others as they run into the woods.

Up ahead, another hunter howls.

16

Reid changes course as soon as he hears the howl, whistling to the others to follow. They listen, at least that is something. He begrudges the need for sound, knowing it will help the hunters locate them, but it's too hard in the dark to simply use gestures. Despite his weariness, Reid runs on, grateful for once for his fear because it gives him access to energy he never knew he had.

To his frustration, his familiar tactic does him no good this time. It doesn't seem to matter which way he leads the kids, how much he alters direction. The howling behind him is always answered from directly ahead. From the volume, the hunter is closing in.

Reid remembers something that troubled him, something he thought of before he met the two poachers. About being herded. He has a flashback of Monica spinning and doubling back on her own trail before heading off again. He stumbles to a halt and turns around, almost running into Drew and Trey, retreating and heading back the way they came. No one says a word, but they all follow.

Reid runs on for another minute before he is forced to swerve to avoid a fallen tree. That's when he loses his grip on Carly. He almost forgot she was there with him, clutching his hand. The sudden missing connection between them reminds him. She tumbles, rolling over and over, coming to a thudding halt against the grounded trunk. He turns to go after her without hesitation, but his fear brings him to a sharp stop.

A hunter emerges from the forest and fixes its attention on the weeping girl.

Time stands still. Reid's mind stumbles over one idea after another in the long, hanging second suspended between them. The three of them hover in it, Carly, the hunter, Reid. He feels the line draw in, pulling them tighter and tighter until he can't breathe. The hunter's claws gleam in the moonlight. Carly's tears glitter on her cheeks, huge eyes swallowing Reid whole. He simply stands there, so torn by indecision he is unable to do anything.

When the moment breaks, Reid has no time left to act, nor the strength to get to Carly before the inevitable.

The hunter pounces in one fluid motion while Reid's tortured mind still tries to figure it out. He hears Carly scream, lunges forward to try to save her, only to be yanked off balance and pulled away. His instincts take over again, but only barely. Reid runs, throat tight, eyes welling with moisture as the girl he barely knows dies in silence in the dark.

Reid immediately thinks of Lucy. She must be dead by now, too slow, too weak. There's no way his fragile and needy sister could possibly survive anything like this. A sob rips from his chest, making it hard to breathe. Carly. Monica. Lucy. Around and around in a circle, joined by Mustache and Scar, and the two boys whose names he never knew. So much death and loss and only fear to keep him moving. There has to be more to life again, it can't just go on like this, one endless run until the hunters finally get around to killing him.

He speeds along on autopilot, letting the kids choose their path, forgetting the world he runs through, ignoring the times he stumbles and almost falls, the sounds and smells of the forest, the gnawing hunger in his stomach. He stops when they make him, runs when they urge him on. Reid is lost inside himself for a long time and can't find a way out again. Doesn't want to, really. It's safer to hide inside himself. He's never been a quitter. His father would be so disappointed, he knows that. But there is only so much Reid's mind can take and he has reached his limit.

The rising light of the sun brings him back to the present and the moment. He curses the warmth of morning for pulling him out of limbo. The other kids try to talk to him, to keep him with them, but Reid doesn't hear their words, not really. Every sound hits him like a muffled whine. He finds a place to collapse and huddles by himself, well apart from the others, shaking from weariness. His leg muscles jump and twitch under his hands. He lets himself sink down, back against a tree, to watch the sunrise and wish he were dead.

In that moment, Reid would gladly trade places with Carly. Wishes it had been him. She relied on him, and he let her down. Let her go. He can never, ever forgive himself. He runs over the whole thing in his mind, the freeze-frame examination driving him deeper and deeper into despair. Reid feels her hand in his, the slickness of her skin, how her palm and fingers just slid out of his grasp as he swerved.

He tried so hard to pull her along with him. He should have held her more tightly, but he didn't. Reid let her go and she fell and rolled away into the darkness and the hunter killed her.

It is all his fault.

He feels Leila's hand on his shoulder but he shrugs her off.

"It's not your fault." She's reading his mind. He looks up and sees her for the first time in the light. She is very pale from her skin to her almost white hair to her clear blue eyes. She stands in front of him, between him and the sun. The glow of it makes her look like an angel. But despite the comparison he refuses to allow her to absolve him.

"I know. I did what I had to do. I left her behind." He is such a liar. But he can't let the others know what he does in his heart. That he could have saved Carly if he had just acted in time. Could have. Should have.

All his fault.

"You would have died too." She sees right past him, obviously. Time to be more harsh, to get his message across.

"Just leave me alone." It emerges in a half-growl out of his dry throat. He is satisfied with the raspy quality of it.

He sounds dangerous, like a lone wolf. That's what he needs to be from now on. No more thinking of others. The realization is so clear to him it chases away the guilt and shame and drives him further into anger.

She waits a moment before doing as he asked. The tiny part of him that still feels human wishes she would come back while the rest of him draws itself around him like a shield and reminds him they left him behind once. Another good reason to go it on his own again. It's not like he can trust them anyway. Why is he so broken up over a girl who would have abandoned him in a heartbeat if it meant her survival?

Drew tries next. Reid hears the distinctive shuffle of the chubby boy's feet. No sneakers but penny loafers. How pathetic.

Still, his message cuts to the bone. "I know what it's like. I felt that way when we left you in the cave. I'm so glad Leila went back for you."

Reid spins, despising the confession. Drew is only grateful because Reid saved his miserable life. How dare he compare who he is to what Reid has become? So what, he left Reid behind. At least no one died.

The look on his face sends Drew back two steps. "You don't get it. I don't give a crap. You hear me?" He is shouting and doesn't care. Let the hunters come. What does it matter? "Just stay the hell away from me."

Drew retreats to huddle with the others. Milo shoots Reid a nasty look and flips him the finger. Reid ignores the skinny kid and goes back to his private hell. Time to get out of there and move on. He can't be responsible for them. Can't. They're just getting in his way, holding him back, keeping him from his chance at winning free of this insanity.

He won't survive another loss.

Reid is on his feet and moving off before he can think twice or talk himself out of it. It takes Leila almost a minute to catch up. When she does her cheeks are flushed and not just from the exertion. She spins him around by her grip on his arm, surprisingly strong for her size.

"Where are you going?"

He doesn't answer. It's pretty obvious to him as it is to the others, from the looks on their faces. They've all followed him. Reid can't have that. But they gang up on him, appealing to the part of him that has shrunk to a fragment under the constant stress.

The part of him that cares what happens to them.

"Please, Reid." Drew is there, too, holding his other arm with one hand while his free one hitches up his pants. "Don't leave us."

"Whatever," Milo mutters. Reid doesn't say anything. There is nothing to say. "Let him go," Milo says. "We don't need him."

"I do," Trey whispers. He is shivering. "He kept us alive last night."

"Not all of us." Milo's lower lip shoots out, his dark eyes locked on Reid, anger vibrating through him. Reid almost tells the boy he agrees with how he feels. But instead of coming out as grief, it emerges as anger.

"I don't want to be responsible for you." He meets Leila's eyes. "Especially when I don't know if I can trust you."

Drew draws a breath. "I deserve that."

"You all do." Reid pulls free of both of them. This lashing out is wrong. He needs to apologize, beg them to forgive him for letting Carly go when all he had to do was hold onto her a little longer, but its easier to blame and rage and be an asshole than face his guilt. "Can you honestly tell me that if you're given the choice to survive but it means one of us dying you won't take it?"

Drew starts to protest but fall silent. Milo's face crumples. Even Leila is quiet.

"Yeah," Reid says. "Thought so."

"I'd like to think not." Leila's whisper carries. "But I really don't know. Is that wrong?" She looks up at him again. "That we don't know for sure? How can we until we're faced with it?"

Reid jerks his gaze away from hers. "We're all on our own out here." He starts walking again. Hears them behind him. Turns and confronts them. Even Milo is there. "You'll be fine without me. Right, Milo?" The boy mutters something and looks away.

"We'll just keep following you." Leila crosses her arms over her chest. "You can't stop us."

Reid lets out a breath of air and rolls his eyes. "Fine. Do what you want." The fragment swells inside him and he is surprised to recognize a feeling of relief. But he has no intention of letting them near him emotionally again. Ever.

Reid continues on and they join him in silence. That only lasts a short time. Drew is beside him suddenly, struggling to keep up but smiling at him like they are friends or something.

"So what does the fence look like? How much power, could you tell? Man, I hope those guys had some food at their camp."

The chubby boy's cheerfulness is obscene and feeds Reid's anger. How can he smile? Or think about his stomach?

Reid's belly growls in protest at being ignored. It just makes him angrier.

"Maybe they left weapons behind too, did you think of that? Or a tent. Soap." Drew groans in joy. "I'd love to be clean. Clothes!" He almost bounces in place as he hurries, shorter legs fighting to match pace. "Do you think?"

Reid's thin patience snaps without much prodding. "You might want to shut the hell up. So the hunters don't hear you."

Drew's smile drops off his face so fast that if the circumstances were different it would have been comical. The chubby boy hangs his head, eyes darting from side to side. "Sorry," slips out of him at a whisper. He keeps step with Reid for only another moment, as though he knows he isn't welcome but doesn't want to go, before falling quietly back.

Reid glances over his shoulder, sees Leila's arm go around the boy and grinds his teeth. She meets his eyes, hers expressionless. Her disappointment hides there behind the blankness in her gaze and Reid shrinks from it.

He's gotten so used to being alone that having the others there is a growing irritation. Every shuffled footstep, every muted cough is a jab to his senses. When they whisper among each other, he wants to wring their necks. Reid is on the verge of turning on them and telling them all to be quiet when he catches a glimpse of what he's been searching for just up ahead.

His heart instantly lifts, the others forgotten. Reid picks up speed and, within moments, is standing in front of the fence.

17

His annoyance is gone. All that matters now is the fence and the promise of freedom it offers. Reid welcomes the familiar feeling of it, the hum vibrating through his sneakers and making his skin break out in goose bumps. He rubs the hairs at the back of his neck and grins with goofy enthusiasm at Drew who smiles right back, previous conversation instantly forgiven.

"Wow," Drew says, glasses winking, "you weren't kidding. This sucker would kill a deer. No pulse, either, steady current. That's unusual." He takes another step closer to it before falling back with a shudder. "What is it, fifteen feet high?" Drew spins in a circle. "And no trees close to it."

Reid realizes the boy is right. "So no chance of jumping over it."

Drew nods. "Exactly. And we don't have the tools to cut one down, so…" he trails off. "Too bad. If we could find a way to sever the connection, the whole thing would lose power."

"What do you mean?" Milo is running his hands over his bare arms and staring at the giant barricade.

"That's how electricity works." Drew suddenly reminds Reid of a teacher he had last year. But there is nothing arrogant about the way he talks to Milo, unlike Mr. Rupert. "You have to have a complete circuit or the power won't flow."

"You think that's what those poachers did?" Milo steps back to stand beside Trey.

"Not likely," Drew says, grunting softly as he bends to pick up a pinecone. He throws it at the chain link. It erupts into a cascade of sparks and bounces off, smoking where it lies on the ground. "If that was the case, the fence wouldn't be live anymore."

"So how?" Reid turns to Drew. "How would they get over?"

Drew's glasses receive an adjustment while he thinks about it. "I don't know," he says at last. "There shouldn't be a way. I mean, maybe they have some kind of tech that allowed them to only disrupt part of the current so they could cut a hole in it, but if so that's more science fiction than science fact." He looks so serious, so grown up. Definitely a teacher. Destined to be one. If they ever make it out of here.

"I'm less worried about how they got in," Reid says, "than how they planned to get out."

Drew turns to Reid. "What do you mean? Isn't it the same thing?"

"Maybe not." Reid looks up and down the line of the fence, seeing it curve away in the distance. "And maybe so. I've been thinking there has to be a gate."

No one says anything, but Drew is nodding. Reid starts to follow the line, knowing they will be right behind him. "Whoever put us in here had to get in somehow, right? That means a gate. Maybe more than one."

"Makes complete sense," Drew says. "They have to have somewhere to run the gennies that keep the fence going, where the capacitors are. And you're right, it's not like we were air lifted in. I remember a van, being carried."

Something about what Drew says triggers a thought in Reid's head, but he loses it before he can figure out what it means. Instead he runs on, hearing his weary band panting along behind him.

He almost misses the camp, it's that well camouflaged. But his eyes are now trained to see everything, miss nothing, knowing his life depends on it. Reid slides to a halt in front of a large draped sheet and thinks of Mustache and Scar.

"A ghillie net!" Drew's excitement is catching. They all move forward, sliding under the edge of the artificial canopy, heavy with fake leaves and branches, a perfect match to the trees around it. Inside the gloom it takes them a moment to adjust to the light, but Reid has no doubt he has found the poacher's camp.

A quick search of camo-colored backpacks turns up fresh clothing and everyone takes advantage. They are too large, but with some liberated rope for belts and ties they manage to get everyone outfitted in something clean. Only Leila turns down a pair of pants, keeping her old jeans but accepting a clean t-shirt from Reid's hands with a small smile.

"There has to be food," Drew mutters to himself. "Has to be."

It's Trey who spots the box high above in the tree. Reid gives him a boost to the lowest branch and within moments the dark painted crate lowers toward them. Trey's yelp of surprise is all the warning they get. Reid grabs Drew who stands directly below, narrowly saving his life when the heavy wooden box comes crashing down.

"Sorry," Trey whispers, holding up his hands. They look very red. "It was heavier than I thought." The last bit of rope snakes to the ground, painted with Trey's blood.

Reid helps him down while Drew, Milo and Leila go through the smashed box. When Reid turns, Trey safe on the ground, he hears an odd snuffling sound and it isn't until he gets closer that he realizes what he's hearing. The three kids are stuffing themselves.

He resists the urge to laugh, pulling them back one by one, liberating a large chunk of power bar from Drew's desperate hands.

"Take it easy," he says. "Trust me." Leila looks up at him, cheeks distended like a squirrel's. She nods, chews a few times, swallows hard.

Trey dives in and Reid is forced to pull him back, too. His own belly demands food, but he remembers the agony of cramps and wants to save them that.

It's not long before the four are groaning and clutching their stomachs. Reid passes around the water bottle while he carefully eats some food of his own. He has at least had some nourishment in the last two days, so his system doesn't rebel quite as much as it did.

Drew turns away just in time, puking up everything he ate. Reid is angry and disappointed and amused all at the same time at the amount of food the boy throws up. Drew sits back, wiping his mouth with his hands.

"Sorry," he says. "I've never been so starving."

Reid hands him a fresh bar. "Slowly." He looks around at the others who are recovering from their own cramps. "One bite at a time."

Reid tosses Trey a first aid kit and watches for a moment as Leila helps him clean and bandage his hands. He returns his attention to the stash, packing up what he can of the food in a backpack he finds near a rolled-up sleeping bag. He would love to take it with him but knows they have to stay light and keep moving. Reid also uncovers a knife, a curved hunting blade, tucked neatly in a leather sheath. He offers silent thanks to Mustache and Scar for leaving it behind.

He is on his feet and ready to move while the others are just settling in.

"We have to go." Reid doesn't wait for them but heads out.

He hears them scramble behind him, the tug of someone's hand on his sleeve. Reid turns to look down at Trey.

"Can't we stay?" The boy has been so quiet Reid is surprised he is the one to speak up, a slip of a kid all huge begging eyes and coffee colored skin etched with dirt. His light voice carries, the plea in it enough to soften even Reid's hardened heart. "Just for a little while?"

Reid wishes they could. Would love to curl up in one of those sleeping bags himself and just pretend he was camping with his dad. But their reality is harsh and their pursuers could be right behind them.

"I'm leaving now," he says. "Stay or come with me, it's up to you." Reid pulls free of Trey's bandaged hands as gently as he can and walks away, the heavy pack full of food on his left shoulder, the comforting weight of the knife down the back of his pants.

He makes it to the other side of the camp before he sees something that makes his heart fall into the bottoms of his shoes. That something flaps and flutters in the bushes. Dark green fabric. He approaches, fingers the silken feel of it. Drew is beside him, mimicking him.

"Parachutes." Drew steps back. Looks up. "Makes sense."

It does. And it breaks Reid's heart. Drives his fury to the forefront of his mind. The cheaters. Cheaters! They flew in. So there is no way out after all.

Drew must know where Reid's thoughts are going because he lays one hand on his arm and squeezes. "They had to have a plan. Parachutes are one way."

It makes him feel a little better. Of course, Drew is right. But how? How were they getting out?

"Maybe they had a ride lined up?" Drew looks around. Points. "Is that a clearing?"

Reid follows Drew for once, all the way to the edge of the trees. Drew called it right. Ahead is a large meadow, empty and serene.

"Just asking for a helicopter to land." Drew grins at Reid. "You know what this means?"

It takes Reid a moment to register. When it does, he almost drops the backpack. A helicopter? Can it be true?

"They left all their things behind," Drew says, logical, precise, and Reid wonders how he has survived without fear being so much a part of him as it is the rest of them. "Which means they were coming back. And this clearing is the closest to their camp."

Reid could hug the chubby boy. Shout to the treetops. Of course. *Of course.* All they have to do is wait.

"Unless they've been and gone." Milo is staring at the sky, arms crossed over his chest. Reid hates that the boy's pessimism is instantly catching.

Drew shrugs, looks around. "Don't see any sign of that. Grass is undisturbed. No flattening, no debris. Helicopters kick up a lot of wind."

Someone's hand slides around Reid's bicep. He looks down and into Leila's face. For the first time since he met her, he sees hope and how beautiful she would be if she weren't so scared.

"Reid," she whispers. "He's right."

He *is* right. To prove it, Drew cocks his head to one side and holds up his hand for quiet. At first Reid doesn't hear anything and almost asks Drew what he is listening to. When he catches the breath of sound, when they all do, Reid's blood surges with joy.

Whump-whump-whump. He's heard it enough times on TV and in the movies to recognize it. Whump-whump-whump. The unmistakable rhythm of helicopter rotors.

Reid scans the sky, not alone in the search, desperate for a glimpse of their salvation. Milo is the first to spot it, shouts, "There!" Points. They all look, see the glitter of sun on glass, watch the bug-like flying machine clear the trees and head their way. All the while the sound gets louder. Reid is suddenly jumping up and down, screaming and waving, happiness and relief washing away his fear. The others are too, tears pouring down their faces. Rescue, so close, so real, is theirs.

Another sound joins their celebration and the steady beat of the helicopter's engine. A high-pitched whine pierces Reid's ears, trailed by a hiss. As they watch, something streaks across the sky toward the hovering aircraft, hitting it dead center.

The helicopter hovers one more moment after impact, a frozen snapshot of freedom. Then, it explodes outward in a ball of flame and smoke. It pitches sideways, a drunken tilt taking it over, before it plummets toward the ground.

Directly at them.

Reid is still screaming, but in terror this time. He pulls Leila along, dragging her as she stumbles and falls, shrieking and sobbing her denial. Drew staggers to Reid's side, takes Leila's other hand and helps him pull her clear and into the woods just as what remains of their salvation slams into the ground with enormous impact, shaking the earth so hard it knocks them to their knees.

Reid holds Leila close as she empties her grief onto his chest, staring at the wreckage, flinching when a second explosion rips it apart. A rotor breaks free, zings toward them. It embeds in the tree above their heads, shaking it so hard they have to dodge the top when it snaps off. They scramble to escape it in the midst of a hail of needles and broken branches.

Reid shakes himself, gets to his feet, pulls Leila and Drew up. Trey and Milo pop into view a few feet away, eyes huge, faces sheathed in tears. Reid builds fresh walls around his heart as he stands there, staring at the wreckage, cursing inside, furious he allowed his hopes to get the better of him.

Of course there is no rescue. Of course whoever kidnapped them is ready for any such attempt. They are trapped and only have each other in the end.

Reid turns to his companions, ignoring the stench of burning fuel and the sizzling pop and crackle of the fire behind him.

"The hunters will come to check this out," he says. "We need to go."

He waits for them, but only for a moment. It's just long enough. They get themselves together and follow. But when he glances over his shoulder one last time, he sees Drew staring at the remains, shoulders shaking. When the boy turns back, Reid recognizes the hate in his face and nods to him.

That's all they have left.

Reid secures the pack on both shoulders and sets the pace. They run on.

18

Despite his resolve, Reid can barely stand to leave their wrecked salvation behind. He's not the only one. He catches the sound of weeping among the others, the occasional wheezing sob cutting through their panting as they follow him back into the forest.

The fence isn't safe now. Not for a while, anyway, he figures. The hunters will find their trail and keeping to the fence will only make it easier for them to hunt the kids down. He regrets leaving it, certain he is right about a gate, an exit, but is determined to keep the barrier's position firmly fixed in his sense of direction so he can track it again.

"That was a missile." Drew has somehow managed to keep up with Reid. From the huffing and puffing the kid is doing the effort is costing him, but they can't afford to slow down. "I'm sure of it. Surface-to-air. Anti-aircraft. Freaking military issue."

It actually takes Drew a few minutes to pant out those short sentences in between gasps of air. When he is done, Reid slows and stops, turning to look at the chubby kid. He tries not to feel sorry for his cherry-red face and the sweat streaking down his cheeks to soak the collar of his stolen t-shirt.

"Military." Reid's mind flashes to the duffle bag, the cabin. Could the army be involved? Was Drew right and this is an alien invasion or something?

Drew's head is bobbing as he gulps breath after breath, glasses fogging around the edges. "I'm sure of it."

"And how would you know, smart ass?" Milo's attitude is getting on Reid's last nerve. But before he can shoot the kid down, Drew does it for him.

"Because I studied about it. Duh."

Reid can't help it. He laughs. There is so little to laugh about, but Drew's casual brush off triggers Reid's funny bone. He starts laughing and can't stop. He finds himself doubled over, gripping his sides, barely able to catch a breath as his stomach aches from the pressure. Tears well in his eyes, spill over his cheeks. When he is finally able to breathe again, his laughter echoes back from the trees.

He hears the others laughing around him and absorbs as

much of it as he can. Trey snorts air as he giggles in a tiny voice. Drew's laughter is more robust, slightly piercing but full and pure. Leila's sounds like liquid light.

For that brief and shining instant, everything is all right in the world. They are safe and happy normal kids. Even Milo starts to snicker after making a rude face.

"Seriously," Leila recovers first, though Reid sees her dabbing at her eyes with the collar of her t-shirt, "how do you know?"

Drew grins at her. "Seriously," he says. "Are you kidding me? I love this stuff."

That sobers them up. Drew's smile fades. "Well," he says, "I used to, anyway."

"So now we think the army is after us?" Milo's attitude is back, but the edge is gone from his voice and even he looks embarrassed after he finishes speaking.

"No," Drew says. "But someone with access to serious military hardware. Mercenaries, maybe. Hired guns." He turns and looks up at Reid. "I've been thinking about it. And I know you guys are right, this is no alien invasion. But, maybe it's an experiment of some kind."

"Great experiment." Milo helps hold up Trey who has started shaking and can't seem to stop.

"Guinea pigs," Trey whispers. There is still humor in his voice but not the nice kind. When he looks up his lips are twisted into a grimace, eyes full of madness. "Mice in a maze. Food for thought." He starts to giggle again, body twitching. Leila rushes to help Milo while Reid just watches, Drew by his side. "Freaking lab rats!"

No one says anything. Reid hates to admit it, but is pretty sure Drew is right. Why else the fence, the secret drop offs of the kids in the middle of the night? The question is, what's the experiment and how much longer will it run?

The idea that they are almost at the end of it first makes Reid hopeful before dashing him down to darkness again. There is no way of knowing. Besides, if it is almost over, the likelihood that whoever brought them there will just let them go is idealistic at best and damned gullible at worst. Chances are, like most test animals, when the project is over they will be destroyed.

Reid exchanges a look with Drew. From the pinched look on the boy's face they are following the same train of thought.

"We have to get out of here," Drew whispers.

"Now you tell me." Reid actually manages a real smile. "Figure it out then, genius."

They have been at rest long enough that Drew has regained his natural paleness. When he blushes, it's painfully obvious.

"Don't call me that," he whispers, "and I'll do my best."

Seems fair to Reid.

Trey has calmed down and Reid knows it's time to move on. He doesn't have to say a word. Everyone falls in behind him. This time when Drew stays at Reid's side he doesn't mind so much.

They don't make it far. Reid just turns to say something to Drew when he catches a flicker out of the corner of his eye. The hunters are on them. He's failed them for the last time.

Reid opens his mouth to shout a warning, but it sticks in his throat. Not hunters. Kids, like them. At least a dozen of them, sliding out of the forest, surrounding them. Reid spins, looking for an exit, too late. They are boxed in.

He isn't sure why this makes him nervous. They should all be on the same side, right? But his tension only rises as the silent crowd stares him down. He feels his new friends closing in for protection. Someone bumps into him. Reid reaches out, catches Leila's hand. He feels a skinny body press to his back and hears the familiar whimper of Trey's terror. Drew stands his ground, but barely. Reid can feel him shaking.

Milo's voice comes from behind Reid, very close. "Tell me they aren't cannibals."

Reid knows it's supposed to be a joke. But no one is laughing.

The kids are all as dirty as Reid's group, and just as desperate looking. He shakes himself internally. This is a great opportunity. He has nothing to fear from them. When he steps out to talk to them, he is mirrored by one of the other group.

This guy is big, taller than Reid's six feet, heavy dark hair hanging over an angry brow. His nose looks like someone broke it on purpose at some point. He's the only one in the new crowd that doesn't look hungry.

"You're in our territory." Big guy's voice is a hammer on an anvil.

"We'll just keep moving then." Like it's going to be that easy. Reid knows the type. Bully.

Reid catches a dark-haired Hispanic guy watching him, eyes almost black. His scowl is so deep it's devouring his face. Reid returns his attention to the leader as he speaks.

"Better not be bringing hunters to our spot." His chest thrusts out and Reid can't help but be reminded of a gorilla he saw once at a zoo.

"Doing our best not to." Reid's flippant attitude will get

them nowhere, but his anger won't let him be diplomatic. They are on the same side, damn it.

"Heard you punks for miles. Might as well wear signs around your necks."

Reid fights not to roll his eyes. Like that made a whole lot of sense.

"I think you mean noisemakers." It's so hard not to laugh. Drew's done it again. Reid glances to the side and finds his chubby friend right next to him, looking defiant. Reid wonders when he started considering the kid his friend.

"What?" Big guy knows easy meat when he sees it and Drew is a prime target. But before bullyboy can do anything about it, Reid steps in front of his friend, all amusement gone.

"We'll be going then." Despite the guy's size, Reid has been watching him move and knows he's soft. In a fight, he's pretty sure he could win as long as he didn't let Gigantor pin him.

Reid really hopes it won't come to that.

Someone squeals from behind him and he hears Leila say his name in a whisper. Reid spins, keeping the bully in his peripheral vision, and sees two of the surrounding kids have a hold of Trey. One of them pushes the skinny boy and the other bounces him back. A couple of the kids laugh but most are as silent and expressionless as ever.

The Hispanic guy just scowls and stares at Reid.

He has to act. Damn, he didn't want to have to do this. He considers appealing to the pack, to the knowledge that they aren't the enemy. But he is certain bullyboy won't let it slide. From the looks of the other kid's faces, no one is willing to put themselves on the line.

Reid is saved the need to rescue Trey. As one entity, the pack of kids tense before vanishing into the underbrush. Reid doesn't have to think twice, already turning and shoving his friends into the trees. Fortunately the undergrowth is thicker here, more like the brushes and shrubbery he encountered when he first started running, or they would have been out of luck.

As it is, Reid barely has time to push Drew into shelter and tuck himself in before he hears panting and dull footfalls. He risks a look through the tightly growing leaves and spots a kid staggering his way down the trail they just left.

Reid is about to lunge for him when a hand holds him back. Reid scowls at the Hispanic guy who points with one long, thin finger. When Reid looks back, he understands.

There is no saving this boy. A hunter is right behind him. Trailing him almost casually. The kid keeps moving forward, barely managing one foot in front of the other. He looks defeated, broken, but still he forces himself on.

When he trips and falls on his face, Reid's heart bleeds for him. So close, almost within touching distance. The kid's head turns to the side, dirt glued to the sweat that coats his skin. His hazel eyes stare, but he sees nothing. Reid is grateful because the boy's face is pointed right at him.

He can't look away either. Refuses to let the kid die alone. Reid hears a soft sound, the pad of a step and sees a black-clad foot settle beside the fallen boy. In the last moment before the end, awareness returns and the kid's eyes lock on Reid's with purpose. He has nothing to offer but his attention, his presence. The boy's naked gratitude outshines his fear.

A whoosh of air, a squeak of sound from his mouth and his light goes out, draining slowly until the last spark is extinguished.

But the horror isn't over yet. The kid is flipped over as two more pairs of feet join the first. There is a tearing sound, the ground flooding with a rush of blood. The hunters crouch, just inside Reid's vision, and begin to stuff raw, steaming bits into their mouths.

He can't react. It's impossible to even comprehend. Milo's cannibal joke returns, still humorless but at least relevant. He tries to look away at last, but is locked in the horror of the truth. Not just hunters, but devourers, eaters of their flesh. It drives Reid's mind to the edge of madness.

Someone cries out, leaps from the bushes and bolts. It pulls Reid out of his spiraling descent into the black. He sees a familiar pair of sneakers on the trail, army pants tied at the ankles with yellow rope. One of the hunters leaps, is gone in a flash, lands next to the fleeing shoes. A voice Reid knows shrieks, body dragged to the kill site. Forced to his knees into Reid's view. Trey screams over and over, barely drawing breath. There is a chuffing sound, like laughter. And then, another whoosh of air and a groan so mournful it takes Reid's breath away. Trey falls to the path, his coffee-colored face washed pale in death.

Reid is forced to huddle there in total silence while the hunters eat his friend, too.

It's not long before they seem satisfied. They rise and grab the bodies, dragging them away down the path. Reid watches them go, wishing they would hurry so he can turn and throw up.

Just as they vanish down the trail, the hunter in the rear spins and looks right at Reid, flashing him a smile, teeth red with blood. Then they are gone into the forest. It takes him a heartbeat to move, but when he does, it's not to puke, but to punch the tree he rests against.

They knew. The hunters. All along. They knew the kids hid there and did nothing about it. Reid is so furious he hits the tree again, feels the skin of his knuckles part, the bones protest. He pulls himself free of the brambles, aching to fight back, knowing at last he was right, that this is a game to the hunters and the kids are just toys.

19

The first person Reid encounters when he hits the path is bullyboy. His rage instantly refocuses as he side steps the puddle of blood his friend left behind and finds a nice, ripe target.

Reid doesn't get a chance to take that anger out on the other guy. Instead, the kid grins at Reid like it's funny and gives him a punch in the arm. Reid is so startled by the change in attitude his fury melts away, leaving only grief behind.

"Joel," the bully jerks a thumb in his own direction. "You guys did good just then. Maybe we can help each other."

Reid can hear Drew whispering behind him. Leila answers back, but their words are lost. He still sees the boy's staring eyes, Trey's dead face. And in front of him, Joel. It's hard not to blame. But Reid's been down that road and knows it won't do any of them any good. Even if it feels like the only thing to do.

"Reid." He doesn't move or gesture but as he speaks the

other's names he feels them come forward to be recognized. "Drew, Leila. And Milo." He catches Leila's short nod out of the corner of his eye, Drew's scowl. Milo slips a little and looks stricken. Reid can't think about it but knows he's slid in the cooling blood.

"We need to move on." The dark-haired Hispanic guy won't meet Reid's eyes anymore. He instead speaks directly to Joel.

"Yeah, right. Let's move out." Joel shoots Reid another smile, a shark's version of humor. Reid's dislike grows by the moment. He almost ducks out and retreats the other way, knowing his friends will follow him. But, his curiosity wins instead and he goes after the bully.

The pack falls in without a word, stumbling and dragging themselves along, stealing peeks at Reid and the others. He ignores them, focusing on the bulky leader.

"This is Marcus." Joel punches the Hispanic guy in the arm. Must be his favorite thing to do. Reid catches Marcus watching him and refuses to look away first. He doesn't have long to wait before the other shifts his gaze.

"He's my second," Joel says like he's some kind of general. "Got to keep these kids in line, you know?"

Reid is more interested in staying alive, but doesn't say anything.

"Where are we going?" Drew is beside Reid and Joel doesn't look happy about it.

"What you want to know for?" Joel barely looks at Drew.

"You said this was your territory," Drew says. "And since you seem to have a purpose, I'm guessing you're taking us somewhere."

Joel barks out a laugh, nudging Marcus. A few of the other kids laugh too, but they look like they are only doing because it's expected of them. The crushed spirit in their eyes is horrible, almost as bad as the blankness of death.

"You hear him? Nice little way of speaking you got there, pudge."

Reid's stomach clenches. Even when he was popular he couldn't stand it when kids were bullied. His father had to pick him up from school a number of times for fighting, but never punished him because he knew what Reid did. He was always on the right side.

Drew never missed a step. "Thank you. Now, are you going to tell us where we're going?"

Reid's respect for his friend takes a leap. Especially when he is sure the boy knows Joel is the kind of bully who will take it out on Drew physically and not think twice about it.

"You'll see, pudge." Joel meets Reid's eyes, a dark and nasty smile on his face.

"Drew." Reid's correction is soft, smooth like melted butter. Joel's eyes widen. But he gets the point. And lets it go.

"There's something you'll want to see."

Joel and Marcus pull out ahead and Reid lets them. Drew waits until they are out of earshot.

"Thanks." His fingers are busy with his glasses. "It's okay, though. You don't have to do that. Not like it's never happened to me before."

Reid doesn't say anything for a moment, trying to come to terms with that. He had a hard time himself this year at school, something he wasn't used to. But being a foster kid carries a kind of stigma he wasn't able to shake no matter how good he was at sports.

"You're my second," Reid says at last. "And no one treats you like that."

Drew's smile is the first good thing Reid's seen in a while.

Leila's hand catches his, squeezes, lets go. Reid almost turns to her, but Joel is shouting for him up ahead. Reid winces from the volume, wondering why, after Joel's comment about noise, he isn't careful with his own.

He joins Joel and Marcus with Drew right beside him at the edge of a cliff. He hears Drew's sharp intake of breath and almost tells the boy to go back with Leila. But one look and Reid feels a surge of pride to go along with that warm feeling he's allowing himself. Drew faces down his fear of heights with barely a tremor in his hands and doesn't look away.

That covered, it still takes Reid a bit to figure out what they are looking at.

"Lots of interesting stuff here," Joel says like it's a supermarket he plans to rip off. "If you're not squeamish." He laughs again, but this time he laughs alone.

Reid's brain makes the connection at the same moment Drew whispers, "Oh my God."

It's a deep, narrow valley and looks manmade, the sides sloped, the dirt fragile from depressions left behind by rain, cuts running from the top down to the bottom of the pit. Inside it are bones, piles of them. Hundreds of kids. Beneath those, charred earth where more have been burned to ash. Hundreds more. Reid feels his bile rise, touch the back of his throat.

"They leave us everything," Joel says as he starts to slide down the side. "Clothes, shoes, you name it." He looks up at

Reid, that darkness still visible, hurtful because the malice is so happy. "Coming?"

Reid joins him, Drew on his heels, breathing heavily as he struggles with his fear. Reid tries once to help, but Marcus is watching and Drew waves him off. He's right. They can't show weakness, not now. Not with these kids.

Once on the bottom, it's not so bad. He can pretend the bones are sticks, they are so clean and white. The scent of char and old smoke disguises any remaining hint of decay. Reid shies from wondering how the skeletons have been stripped like that while his practical side goes digging for things he can use.

His sneakers, for instance. They weren't new to begin with and all the running over rough terrain has worn them almost completely through. He spots a pair nearby, checks the size. Perfect. The jeans and t-shirt neatly piled next to them would fit him too, but Reid isn't willing to go that far even as he wonders why they aren't covered in blood.

It's like the hunters left them gifts but make them walk among their dead to receive them. The longer Reid is in the pit the more his horror grows and he finally scrambles out with his friends on his heels while Joel and the others follow more slowly.

Marcus is the first to point out the backpack. "What did you find?"

Reid's first instinct is a sharp jab of anxiety. He doesn't want to say. There are too many of them and he fully intends to abandon this group the first chance he gets. He and his friends need all the food they have for their own survival. But Milo speaks up before he has a chance to mutter an answer.

"We found a camp. Power bars and stuff." Reid wants to throttle him. Milo instantly knows he's made a mistake because he turns with a look so full of remorse Reid forgives him.

Joel is beside Reid in a flash, the others hovering around. "Food? You going to share that?"

Like he has a choice, now. Reid hands out bars. When the last kid clutches his to his thin chest, the backpack is almost empty. Joel tries to take it but Reid slings it back over his shoulders and glares. The bully backs off, grinning and chewing. Reid almost comments when Joel takes a bar from one of the smaller kids, pushing the skinny girl aside, and eats it, too. Reid holds his peace, however. He can't save them. Has no desire to. His only concern is protecting what remains of the food. And his friends.

"So, I'm working on a plan." Joel speaks around a mouthful. No one looks up. But Reid can feel their tension and wonders about it. Marcus steps forward but Joel shoves him off. "No one agrees with me." There is food in his teeth and again Reid gets the impression he's been eating on a regular basis while the rest of them look starved.

"I'm listening." Can't hurt.

"We set a trap, see? For one of the hunters. Send a runner out, use him as bait. Lead the bastard into a spot we can surround." He hocks up a wad of phlegm and spits it out, barely missing Milo's sneaker. "Found the perfect place just this morning, in fact."

"And then?" Drew's being cocky, but Joel doesn't give him a hard time. Just smiles that horrible smile.

"Then the rest of us kill the some bitch," he says. "Take the fight to them."

"With what?" Drew rolls his eyes at Reid. "Sticks and stones?"

Joel finally looks pissed, but it's okay with Reid. He prefers the bully's anger to his dark humor.

"Yeah, sticks and stones! We sharpen them, right? Lay in wait and BAM!" A couple of the kids jump. "Dead hunter."

"I see several flaws in your so called plan," Drew says while Reid thinks it over. "One, what if the hunter catches the kid before we can spring the trap? Two, don't you think they are smart enough to smell something like this and not fall for it?"

"Worth a try, I say," Joel shoots back. "Who asked you, pudge?" His eyes flicker to Reid and he grins. "Sorry, *Drew*."

"Besides," Drew goes on, speaking to Reid as if Joel doesn't exist. The fact is not lost on the pack leader and his anger returns, smoldering. "We'll just piss the hunters off. They'll come after us even worse then."

Something about Joel's idea has sparked a light in Reid and he shakes his head. "It might work."

Joel sits back and laughs, punching Marcus in the arm. Reid reminds himself not to stand too close to the bully. His right shoulder is still giving him trouble. "There, you see? Reid agrees." He looks around at all the kids. No one meets his eyes, but a handful murmur how great that is.

Not for the first time, Reid wonders about Joel and what he's done to these kids.

He shoves that aside for now. The idea of striking back, of getting even a small measure of revenge, is worth collaborating with the bully.

"How many are there?" Leila's voice is so soft and unexpected everyone looks at her. She's one of the few females in the group. Girls must be easier to catch, Reid figures. But not her. He wouldn't count her out before himself.

"How many what, sweetheart?" Joel's attention is very unwelcome. Reid makes it plain the bully should back off by simply taking her hand.

"Hunters." There's an edge to her voice, now. "How many hunters, smart ass."

Joel looks like he wants to make another comment, one Reid is sure will start a fight. Instead he shrugs. "No one knows."

"Have you tried this brilliant plan of yours before?" Drew is so skeptical even Marcus pays attention, though his face stays stony and blank.

"Nope," Joel says. "Just came up with it, like I said. 'Cause of the perfect spot and all." He belches and scratches his stomach through his filthy shirt. Reid wonders why he doesn't help himself to a fresh one. "Need a fast runner to make it happen." Joel's eyes are fixed on Reid's. "Someone they won't catch too easy."

"Are you volunteering?" Leila's hand tightens. Reid can feel the warning in that squeeze.

"Nope, not me," Joel says. "Can't run that fast. But I can swing a rock like a some bitch."

Some bitch is Joel's favorite swear, obviously. Reid feels Marcus staring at him and turns to face him. Marcus looks away, but not before something in his eyes triggers Reid's anxiety. Not everything about this situation is as it appears. And yet, the plan has a chance if he is willing to risk it.

"I'll do it," Reid says.

20

Reid decides to wait until full nightfall. He is tired and needs to rest. His friends huddle around him as he doles out the last of the food, taking the final bar for himself. Leila tries to hand hers back to him but he shakes his head.

"We'll all need our strength, I'm thinking."

She nods, but doesn't eat. Her pale eyes flicker over to the others. They are all sprawled out near the lip of the hole, Joel laughing over something he's said to the dark and silent Marcus who simply stares at Reid's little group.

"I don't trust him." Leila reaches for Reid's hand again, but pulls back before they touch. "Please, can't we just go?"

"Where?" Reid forces himself to swallow a bite despite it sticking in his throat. Her mention of leaving has made his fear rise. She's right. They could just run off. No one in Joel's pack could catch them if they really wanted to retreat. But his question remains and Leila looks away.

"Anywhere but here," she whispers.

"I'm with Leila," Drew says around a mouthful of his own. "There's something really wrong with this whole situation. Did you see the hunters, how they acted? They knew we were there."

Milo shudders and slides closer to Reid. "That was messed up. What happened to Trey."

They all take a moment. Reid bows his head and tries to get the dead boy's face out of his mind. It's not working.

"I know." Reid folds the end over his power bar and stuffs the remainder in his pocket, too nervous to eat anything else. "That's why this is important. If we can take one of them out, the kids will know it can happen. It's not the best plan," he stops Drew from interrupting by raising one hand, "but if we can pull it off… Drew, if these kids learn they can fight back…"

"Reid is right." Milo offers a little smile. "I may be a jerk, but I know when you're doing what needs doing." Reid accepts the boy's apology. No one owes him anything.

"How do we know Joel won't double cross us or something?"

Drew tosses his wrapper to the ground with some heat. Leila immediately retrieves it and puts it in her pocket.

"What do you mean?" Reid is so wrapped up in the thought of deliberately baiting a hunter he can't figure out the question.

"He obviously enjoys being the boss around here," Drew says. "And sees you as a threat." Drew glanced at Joel and back again. "I wouldn't put it past him to try to get rid of you."

Reid shrugs. That won't be up to Joel. It won't be the bully chasing after him through the forest with claws for hands and sharp teeth thirsting for his blood. So he doesn't care at the moment.

"Let me do it." Milo's chocolate brown eyes never waver. "I can run as fast as you. Faster maybe."

They all know that's a lie. Reid smiles. "I know," he says, "but if something happens, who will take care of Drew?"

Milo grins, but Drew doesn't take the joke bait.

"I'm serious," Drew says.

"I know." Reid sits back, leaning against a tree-trunk. "But I'm the best one for the job. You've seen his crew. Aside from that Marcus, no one else looks like they could outrun you." Another joke. Reid can't help it. And, finally, Drew smiles.

"Fine," he says. "Then you sleep and we'll watch over you."

"You all need to rest," Reid says. The dark circles under Leila's eyes are worse and even Milo looks ashen despite his dark skin.

"Never mind us," Leila says. "We'll take turns. And we'll wake you when it's time."

Reid is sure he won't sleep, he's so keyed up, but when he allows himself to curl on his side with his friends around him, he is lost to the dark in moments.

He wakes to gentle hands on his shoulder, shaking him. Reid is instantly aware, senses hyper focused. He can smell the mix of stirred earth and crushed spruce needles, the hint of old smoke coming from the pit. The ground is both soft and hard beneath him, the darkness wrapping him up like a blanket. He turns and meets Leila's eyes. She does her best to hide her fear for him, but he can see right past the wall she puts up.

"Joel sent for you," she says.

When he tries to pull away from her she clings on, not tightly, just enough to make him pause. She doesn't say anything else. She doesn't have to. Reid just nods and removes her hands from his arm.

"It'll be okay," he says.

"Promise?" There is a hint of moisture in her eyes. She blinks several times before looking down, fingers twining around the laces of her shoes.

"Promise." He can't, not really and they both know it but she smiles at him for the effort he made.

"You need to do something for me." Reid leans forward, lips against her ear. "Your turn to promise." She doesn't respond so he goes on. "If anything happens to me," he feels her twitch in protest beside him, "I want you to take Drew and Milo and run."

He leans back, meets her eyes. She just nods once and gets to her feet. He stands beside her, turning to look for the others, and comes face-to-face with Marcus.

"This way." It's only the second time Reid's heard the other speak and the first time he paid attention. He was expecting a Latino accent, but Marcus's voice is almost polished English. Like he spent time in Britain or something.

Reid follows him, Leila trailing along behind. He spots Drew and Milo standing apart from the others. When Drew tries to join Reid, Joel holds him back. Reid just stares at the bully and swears to himself he will survive this if only to teach the jerk a lesson.

No one touches Reid's friends. No one.

He wonders at the passion in him, where his need to be alone has gone, his desperate loss of empathy. Everything is different inside him now. Leila's hand squeezes his. She moves to join Milo and Drew as he realizes friendship trumps even the threat of death.

His dad would be proud. He's on the right side again.

"This is the deal." Joel grins at Reid. "You go out there," he gestures into the forest, "and make lots of noise. When you hear a howl, start running back here."

"Where is the trap going to be set?" Reid meets Drew's eyes, silently commanding the boy to be silent while Joel answers his question.

"Right here." Joel opens his arms wide, looking around. "If we can get the thing in the pit, all the better."

"This is too large of an area." Drew scowls, ignores Reid's warning. "A lot can go wrong with this."

"You got a better idea, pudge?" Joel doesn't even pretend to care what Reid thinks of his attitude toward Drew and Reid realizes his friend is right about Joel's goal to get rid of him. Reid decides he's going to be in for disappointment.

"I do, as a matter of fact." Drew walks off and Reid

immediately follows. He sees the surprise in Marcus's face and the anger in Joel's, but ignores them both.

They don't go far. Drew stops in a narrow part of a path, more deer trail than the cleared ways they have gotten used to. "See, it's really sheltered here." He points to exceptionally thick undergrowth. "And these trees are heavy with leaves but climbable." He points upward. "This one is dying." Drew shoves against a gray-barreled tree. It rocks slightly, ready to fall. "Reid leads the hunter here. He passes this spot, we knock down the tree. Won't stop the thing, but should slow it down. Then the rest of us attack from the sides and back and from the trees above. The smaller kids can be up there throwing rocks. That way we corner it and have a better chance." He meets Reid's eyes. "What do you think?"

Reid is so proud he suddenly knows how his dad felt when he did something fantastic. Instead of embarrassing himself and his friend, however, Reid just nods. "Sounds good to me."

He hears Joel grumbling behind him and catches the look of speculation Marcus gives Drew, but in the end everyone agrees and the plan is set.

It doesn't take long for the kids to place themselves and they are almost done before Reid heads out.

"Be careful." Drew shuffles back and forth from foot to foot, eyes on the ground. He seemed so confident when he explained the plan, but now he's like a little kid whose puppy got run over. "We need you, remember?"

Reid squeezes Drew's shoulder with one hand in answer and runs off into the forest. He can't speak. Doesn't trust what might come out.

Reid only goes so far. He wants a good start at the trap and he knows how fast the hunters move. He decides he's going to get some payback one way or another and chooses to shout profanities into the night to summon the creatures in black.

Reid's first curse is barely past his lips when he hears a howl. It's close. Far closer than he'd like. He freezes for a moment, shocked that this is actually working before spinning in his tracks and running with all his strength for the trap.

There is a long and terrifying moment when he is certain he won't make it. He risks a glance behind him and sees the hunter on his trail, so near he can make out the flash of the things claws, the grin on its face as its white teeth shine in the moonlight. Reid has an irrational thought, how the full moon is beginning to wane and what will happen to them when it is new and they can't see anything? But he is running for his life and the answer is irrelevant, entering and leaving his mind so fast it's like the pace he's keeping.

And then he is on the trail and swerving for the underbrush, diving for safety. He hears the hunter chuff behind him, knows he has seconds before those claws gut him. Reid's heart leaps. He's safe! Until his body stops up against something hard. Joel stands over him, grinning down on him, looking almost as evil and alien as one of the hunters.

"He's here!" Joel uses one foot to roll Reid back into the path. Reid is so shocked by the betrayal he lies there and stares into the other boy's eyes while the hunter's breathy chuffing gets closer. Joel laughs. "Enjoy your dinner." With that, he runs away.

Reid scrambles to his feet and faces the hunter. It is still ten or so feet away, but he knows the thing can close the space faster than he can run. His mind flashes to the back of his pants and the weight there. He has a chance after all. If he can act quickly enough.

His hand slides around to the waist of his khakis and feels for the knife he liberated from Mustache and Scar. His fingers find the heavy leather sheath but the blade itself is gone. Reid seizes up, cursing and yelling in his head while he stares at the hunter.

It laughs at him, a horrible sound, its shining silver eyes only glimmers around its massive pupils. It takes its time, easing around him, head cocked to one side, snuffling his scent.

It's hopeless. He is lost. Betrayed. And not the first to be turned over to the enemy, Reid knows it in his bones. This is how Joel has survived. He has made a pact with the hunters, giving up lives for his own worthless existence. It is this knowledge that prevents Reid from quitting. He can't give up. He has to make Joel pay for what he's done and Reid can't do that if he is dead.

Someone screams in the distance. The hunter is distracted. It's brief, but Reid takes it and dives for the bushes. He is up and running as the creature snarls behind him. Reid swerves and weaves, using every trick he can, going on instinct and his will to live, dodging death at every corner. The hunter is right behind him, but can only move so fast in the underbrush. At one point Reid grabs the trunk of a spruce and uses it to leap over a shrub, risking a look over his shoulder.

He was wrong about the hunter's lack of ability to move quickly through the forest. It leaps with immense agility from tree to tree. His own clumsy effort seems pathetic in light of the thing's dexterity. And yet, it hangs back, takes its time.

Plays with its food.

Fine. Reid jumps for the path and lands hard, breath almost gone from the effort. At least he will die running.

Fate is cruel. It snaps out a low branch and hooks his new sneaker. Flings him to the ground face-first, his head bouncing from a protruding root, not enough to harm him really, but just enough to make him see flashes of light. In that moment it takes him to recover, Reid is lost.

He manages to spin over onto his back and see his destiny crouch over him. The hunter breathes its foul breath into his face, right arm rising slowly over its head, the shining claws sparkling in the cold light of the moon.

A lifetime runs through Reid's mind, sunny days with his parents, camping with his dad, playing little league and high school football. The smell of his mother's hair. His favorite stuffed bear. Then, more current memories force his old life aside. Lucy, the apartment. Drew. Milo. Leila. He worries about them in the last half second of his life and hopes she does as he told her. Prays they can escape Joel. He can't bear the thought they will become victims like him.

The hunter's down stroke seems to take forever. It pauses part way to his heart, its eyes growing even wider. Its mouth gapes, sharp teeth dripping saliva onto his face. It jerks forward, face hovering inches from his as something wet and hot pools on Reid's stomach. He glances down. A glistening spike sticks out of the hunter's gut. When he looks back up into the things eyes, he sees the light in them fade just like it had for Trey and the other kid he was forced to watch die. But this time he feels no remorse, no grief. Only shock and, ultimately, fierce joy.

The hunter rears back, a soft cry escaping it as though it can't believe its life is over. The spike jerks free, leaving a gaping hole behind. The hunter twitches once, claws grasping the air.

It dies then, falling toward him. Reid flings up his arms in an attempt to keep it from landing on him, and yet unable to look away. He needn't have bothered. As it collapses, it disintegrates into dust. Reid breathes in some of the glittering powder it leaves behind, choking and gagging on the remains of the creature. For an instant he feels powerful, as though he could take on all the hunters and win. But the moment passes and he forgets about it as he stares up into Leila's eyes.

She is sobbing, face twisted into a grimace she can't control. In her hands she clutches a thick branch, sharpened on one end and glistening with the hunter's blood.

21

It only takes him a moment to recover. Reid leaps up and hugs Leila. The stick drops at their feet and he kicks it violently away.

"We have to go," he says. "Are you okay?"

She nods, manages to stop sobbing, but the tears continue to fall.

Reid clutches her hand and they run together back along the trail. It's Leila who pulls him into the trees at a certain place. He trusts her instantly. His fury burns him up inside, so much he can barely think of anything but what he is about to do to Joel.

They are back with the group so fast he is almost shaken out of his anger by the familiar sight of the pit and the pack. Everyone stares, some kids falling back, but even Joel is in complete shock when Reid runs straight for the bully.

Leila's hand drops away just in time to save her from being dragged into the punch Reid throws.

It takes Joel right on the crest of his nose and sends him flying backward. Reid feels his crusted knuckles rebel, pain flaring, but he doesn't care. He dives for the fallen bully and straddles him, pounding away at the other guy over and over again. Reid is unaware of the other kids or what they are doing, detached from the fear a hunter might come. All he can focus on is the pulp he is creating of Joel's face and the weak and pathetic attempts the bully makes to fight him off.

Someone pulls Reid away. He struggles, a deep growl of fury growing into a roar as he jerks himself free and staggers back. He spins on the one who stopped him and just recognizes Marcus.

"He's done." Marcus glances at Joel. "You've won already. Leave off."

Reid takes a challenging step toward Marcus and bumps his chest with one bloody fist. "Who says?"

Marcus shrugs and backs off a step. "Not saying he doesn't deserve it. Just that there's another way to make sure he pays."

"You knew." Reid is shaking, unable to stop the tremors, his anger's outlet groaning on the ground and no target anymore.

"You freaking *knew* and you let it *happen*."

"It's not like the deal started on purpose." Marcus won't look at him. "Not the first time. Joel just pushed a kid out of hiding. The hunter took him instead. That was the beginning." Marcus grinds to a halt. Reid spins and pins all the kids with his glare, but no one will meet his eyes except his own friends.

"Reid..." Drew trails off.

"He tried to kill me." Reid lashes out with one foot, feeling Joel's ribs give way under the blow. He has never been so furious. Like he's possessed by someone else's rage. "This sick *bastard*," Reid kicks Joel again, rocking the bigger boy's body to the side and getting a groan out of him, "uses kids as *bait* for the hunters so they won't take him. He feeds them *kids*. Like *us*." All of a sudden his stomach cramps and he wants more than anything to be ill, but refuses to let go of his fury just yet.

"I know," Drew whispers. "As soon as you left they corralled us and brought us back here. That's when I figured it out." He wipes at his eyes under the shining plastic of his glasses. "Leila got away, went after you. But we couldn't." He is openly crying now. "But Reid, you can't leave him for the hunters. You can't. You'd be him, then."

Reid knows what Drew is saying, understands the logic, the emotion even. But his heart is hard against the bully and out there is only life and death. There is no middle ground for someone like Joel.

"I don't make the rules," Reid says. "And he's not my responsibility anymore." The anger finally unclenches and eases, his upset belly relaxing at last. "He's on his own."

Reid walks away. Drew is at his right side, Leila at his left. He feels Milo scoot up behind him. As for the others, he doesn't care. A hunter calls nearby. Reid picks up the pace, hands suddenly throbbing.

He doesn't make it far when Leila pulls him to a halt. "We're not alone," she whispers. Reid looks around, not surprised to find Marcus and the rest of the kids trailing along behind.

"I can't be responsible for them, too." Reid tries to turn away but Leila won't let him.

"They need you," she says.

Just behind them Reid hears Joel crying out. They all listen, no one breathing or making a sound.

"Oh God, help me, please, help me! No. No! I fed you! I gave you what you wanted! I gave you what you—" His words cut off, there is a heartbeat of silence. A scream, long and loud and drawn out raises goose flesh on Reid's arms. And then, at last, silence.

Reid waits another moment before speaking. "You cross me or any of my friends and I leave you behind." He is talking to them all, but he keeps his eyes locked on Marcus. "I even suspect you've betrayed us and you're dead. Understand?"

He doesn't wait for an answer. Reid doesn't need one. He is clear. And justice will be done.

They run on for some time, the exercise wearing away the last of Reid's fury. When they finally pull up for a rest, it's because of Marcus.

"The smaller kids can't keep up." He is panting himself, just at Reid's shoulder, barely able to reach him around the suddenly protective Milo.

Reid lets them stop, crouching with his friends while the pack groans and collapses for a bit. "Keep your eyes on them," Reid says. "I know Joel's beaten them down, but he's also taught them to sell each other out. Don't think for a moment they won't do it to us."

"I don't know," Drew says and, not for the first time, his optimism amazes Reid. "They've seen the worst that can happen. I think they'll want your protection too much to screw this up."

"At least you're not going to sacrifice them to the hunters," Milo whispers. "That would make me want to follow you. If I wasn't already."

Reid grinds his teeth. He meant to do something about this whole leader mess. Then Leila speaks up and shocks them all.

"I say we leave them behind right now." She looks so fierce even Reid is a little afraid of her. "We couldn't trust Joel and we can't trust them. Besides, it's easier with just the four of us. A group this size, we're slower and a bigger target for the hunters."

"You want to abandon them?" Drew's mouth hangs open, his braces glittering. "You? There are little kids in that group."

"So?" She tosses back her blonde hair, hanging in dirty strings around her pale face. "If we're going to survive we need to think of ourselves. Us, I mean." She flushes, the pink visible even in the moonlight. "I'd do anything for the three of you."

Reid squeezes her knee. "We know, Leila. And we get it." He sighs. "I don't want them with us either. But I seem to recall telling someone else I wasn't interested and being followed."

Drew grins and ducks his head while Leila offers a little smile.

"So for now, we just keep moving," Reid says. "And if they

follow, well… not much we can do about it. But we're in this together and if something happens to one of them, so be it."

Leila nods right away, but it takes a moment for Milo to agree. He finally does and they all look at Drew. He tosses up his hands. "Fine. Okay. I see your point." He glances at the weary pack behind them. "It's just… I was one of them once."

"I know how you feel," Reid says. "I do. But they have Marcus. He can lead them if it comes down to it. And Drew? You were never one of them. You wouldn't have let Joel sacrifice kids."

That seemed to make Drew feel a little better because he nods as well.

"That's settled," Reid says, "now we need a new plan."

"I've been thinking about that," Drew says. "The way I see it we need water, food and shelter. Or a way out. Right?"

"Preferably a way out," Reid says.

"Right. So, the fence."

The damned fence. Reid has forgotten about it, about the crashed helicopter. Now it comes rushing back. "Yes," he says, "I still think it's the best idea so far."

"Then we find it again," Drew says, "and follow it."

"What about the hunters?" Milo hugs himself in the dark. "Won't they be watching it?"

"We know someone is," Leila says. "Someone with missiles."

"We'll just have to risk it." Drew glances behind him and stiffens. "Marcus."

He is there before the word leaves Drew's mouth.

"We need to talk."

Reid shrugs. "About what?"

"Plans." Marcus looks around the group then back to Reid. "I think we're safe for a short time, but now that Joel is gone the hunters will know the bargain is off. Or they will suspect. He was the one they negotiated with."

Again Reid gets the impression Marcus has a British accent. He is as well spoken as Drew if not better and holds himself like he knows how to fight.

"You could have stopped him." Reid's anger comes back but it doesn't have the same edge it did.

Marcus scowls. "You think it was easy?"

"None of this is easy," Reid snaps back. "But being a coward doesn't make it any easier."

Marcus looks like he's ready to throw a punch and Reid welcomes it. Leila puts an end to the fight before it starts.

"How long?" She focuses on Marcus, drawing his attention.

"A few hours. Maybe half a day."

"How many did he turn over to them?" Reid wishes Drew hadn't asked that question, but part of him needs to know.

"Three, sometimes four a day." Marcus clears his throat. "There are new kids popping up all the time usually. But there haven't been as many lately. It was making Joel nervous. Then you four showed up. He saw it as a sign."

Reid wonders about the drop in numbers. Are the hunters simply getting better at their job or was Drew right about the experiment? Maybe they are near the end. If so, escape is even more urgent. He doesn't want to be there when the hunters decide to cull the last of their food source.

"They knew we were there," Drew says. "Why didn't they just attack? I mean, agreement or not, they don't seem the type to keep a deal to me."

Marcus shrugs. "Don't know. Only that as long as we stay hidden they won't kill us, but if a kid gets caught in the open it's game over."

Reid can't listen anymore. He gets up and walks away, sitting on his own behind a tree, out of the view of the others. His chest tightens with a mix of anger and grief. How is this happening? Why is it happening? He is no closer to answers than the night he was dumped here.

It isn't long before Leila joins him. She doesn't speak, just hugs her knees and rocks slowly back and forth. He's happy she's there once he allows the tension in his body to release. Of all of them, she seems to understand what he needs the best.

When it finally occurs to him she saved his life, he blurts, "Thank you."

"You're welcome," she says. "I hope it makes up for leaving you behind."

"That would be yes," he says. And smiles.

Leila starts to cry, softly, barely making a sound. Reid doesn't think about it, just hooks her around her shoulders with one arm and pulls her against him. She rests her cheek on his shoulder, the fabric soon wet from her tears. He just holds her for a long time while she lets out her own grief.

"You did the right thing," she says, "leaving Joel behind."

She sighs then, and snuggles closer. Before Reid can think of anything to say in answer to that, she relaxes into sleep.

22

He waits for Leila to wake, not wanting to disturb her. She does after a short time, smiling at him as she lifts her head, embarrassment in her face, but gratitude too.

"You didn't have to do that," she says.

"I know." Reid gets to his feet and offers his hand. "But we should be getting back to the others."

As they make their way through the trees, Reid notices something odd. He's become so in tune with the outdoors he can feel the night aging, the coming dawn now so tied into his internal clock he is pretty sure he could predict the moment the sun will come up.

He and Leila find the rest of the group huddled in a miserable clump. They watch him with hurt and frightened eyes, more a pack of wild animals than kids, jumping at the slightest sound, looking far older than they really are, as though the chase has aged them. For all he knows it has, the stress on their bodies so powerful he wonders if some of the weaker ones would recover completely, given the chance. That's the thing, the rub. Given the chance. Reid knows the likely hood of them finding out is almost none.

His empathy rises up again, unbidden and despite his need to keep them out of his heart for his own protection, the side of him his father instilled, the side that took care of those in need, won't let him stay angry. It reminds Reid none of this is their fault. And he knows if he can get them out too, he will.

For some reason that makes him feel a whole lot better. Like a giant knotted hate inside him has eased, the one fed by fear and rage, and the knowledge that someone did this to them on purpose.

When he goes looking for Drew and Milo, he feels a thrill of fear. Neither boy is present. But before he can ask about them, a small kid in ragged jeans speaks up.

"They're gonna know. And they're gonna come after us." His voice shakes so much Reid can barely make out what the boy is saying, but even without catching every word the message is obvious. Now that Joel is gone and the arrangement undone, the hunters will be coming.

They need a plan.

"They'll kill us all if they catch us." That was the little girl Joel stripped of her food. She is so emaciated she's a walking skeleton. Her fear radiates out of her like her body is unable to hold it in anymore.

It almost makes Reid sick to his stomach to look at her. He wishes he stopped Joel from stealing her food. They have to run again and there's no way this little thing, all that remains of a normal girl, is going to be able to keep up.

There's one shot and he knows it. Reid is about to tell them about the fence when Drew puffs his way through the trees and stops next to Leila.

"I found something."

Reid doesn't get to inquire. Marcus makes himself known, pushing his way to his feet and through the kids, already talking.

"We need to offer a sacrifice."

Reid thought he felt sick before. The very idea twists his insides and makes him want to scream. It disgusts him, almost as much as the weakness in Marcus for even suggesting it. He can feel the other guy's fear, has been there himself, but never once considered doing what the rest of the forlorn pack is now nodding in agreement over.

"Never," Reid says. "You heard what I said."

"We have to do something." Marcus paces back but doesn't quit, face a sullen mask. He's not exactly challenging Reid physically. But Reid can feel the pack swaying in his favor. "Or we all die."

"Not that," Reid says. "Never again."

"We didn't make this situation." Marcus looks around at the others, courage feeding from their growing support. "We didn't ask to be brought here. And it's not our fault Joel made that agreement with the hunters. But it's kept us alive so far. It can again, at least until we figure something else out."

Reid is on Marcus so fast the other guy doesn't have a chance to react until it's too late. Reid can feel the hardness of Marcus's muscles under his shirt and wonders why he is such a coward, why he let Joel push him around. "I said no. And I meant it." He shoves Marcus away, not bothering to watch the other guy stagger, but catching the glare he levels at Reid. "We are in this together or we go our own way and you do what you want to each other. Pick one. But you can't have both. I won't allow it."

They are silent long enough for Drew to speak up again.

"Did you want to know what I found or not?" Reid spins to look at his friend and almost laughs at the disgusted look on the boy's face.

"Sorry," Reid says. "Tell or show?"

"Oh, just come on." Drew gestures at Reid and turns, going back into the trees.

Everyone follows, even Marcus, though he stays on the edge of the pack, ghosting through the forest on his own. Reid keeps his distance as well, not trusting the other guy at all. Or his own temper. But now he knows Leila is right. These kids, this group of starving animals, have been taught to sell each other out over and over again. Forced to witness the loss of friends, being told it was for the good of the rest.

How many of them are so twisted up inside they don't understand right from wrong anymore? He's not even sure if there is a way to teach them otherwise now, not out here with the hunters on their trail. It's amazing to him what they made themselves get used to. Their survival has come at the price of the deaths of others and they have grown comfortable with that.

Reid wonders how comfortable Marcus would be if he were chosen to be the sacrifice. Not very. In fact, he's pretty sure there would be an almost instantaneous nomination of someone else. The sad part is, Reid is certain the kids would let him get away with it as long as they got to survive.

He finds himself thinking about Joel, how horrible his life must have been that he found it so easy to make such a bargain. How very little the bully valued other lives. Reid's mind drifts, putting himself in that position, and he has to fight the tightening in his throat as he chokes up at the thought. Who would he choose if it was him? Who would he send as a sacrifice? He looks around him, at Leila, Milo, even Marcus, while his eyes drift over the small, filthy faces of the ones he has yet to get to know. If it was the only way, could he send one of those terrified faces to their deaths?

Reid shudders and jerks himself out of that train of thought. No, of course not. Never.

As a distraction, Reid catches up with Drew. "What did you find?"

"Caves, I think." Drew grins up at him. Reid still finds it hard to believe his friend can be so happy. "I left Milo there to explore. We can hide for a bit, gather some food, find water maybe? Leave the others here while we look for the fence?" He shrugs. "Could be it's a bad idea, but it's something."

Reid punches him lightly on the shoulder. "Good job."

Drew adjusts his glasses, cheeks flushing as he hitches his pants. Reid notices the rope that holds them up is loose again. "Thanks."

Only then does Reid realize the sky is brighter, his friend's face clear. So much for his internal clock warning him about the sunrise. He shrugs it off with a grin of his own. He's been a little too busy to sit around waiting for the sun to come up.

Reid spots the black opening through the trees before he clears them and has an instant moment of recognition.

"A mine."

"What?" Drew glances at him, then at the hole. And face palms. "Of course," he groans. "I'm such an idiot. It's an old mineshaft. Sorry, guess I'm tired."

The mouth is damaged, rough around the edges, so Reid understands how the weary Drew missed the connection in the dark. "How far does it go?"

"Don't know for sure," Drew says. He waves at Milo, who emerges from the hole. Milo waves back, jumping up and down in his excitement. Reid runs to him, the others trailing behind, though when he stops next to the vibrating kid, Leila, Drew and Marcus are right there with him.

"It's awesome!" Milo jerks his thumb back over his shoulder. "Goes on a long way. And there's electricity in there! Lights!"

Reid frowns at that and shares a look with Drew.

"That's not right," Reid says.

"Shouldn't be power," Drew agrees.

"I found something else." Milo seizes Reid's hand and drags him along into the tunnel. "You have to see!"

Reid follows him, hesitant. The opening is dark but the moment he passes over the threshold he sees a glow ahead, faint, but there. After a minute or so walking and stumbling over rocks, he comes to a weak bulb flickering in the darkness. Milo lets go of his hand and points down where a pile of loose dirt and rubble blocks part of the path, casting long shadows back the way they came.

"Think we could use these?"

Drew crouches next to Reid and whistles. A small wooden box lies open, the old slats crushed to splinters. Inside are six slim rods, faded and dusty with age, long buried in the mine. But Reid knows dynamite when he sees it.

"Wow." Drew squints up into the light. "Yes, yes we can. If..."

"If what?" Marcus hovers over them and Reid resents it, but lets it be for the time being.

"If the compound hasn't be compromised. There's no way of telling how old this stuff is." He doesn't touch it, just looks closer. When Milo reaches for a stick of it, Drew slaps his hand away. "I wouldn't. Not just yet. It could blow up in your face."

Milo snorts like Drew is full of crap, but Reid notices the boy backs off to a healthy distance.

"Wicks are still attached. And the casings look undamaged." Drew grins at Reid. "They could be okay."

"For what?" Marcus hasn't backed off. Reid thinks it's time he did and stands abruptly, spinning on the other guy and forcing him back just by walking toward him, his shadow retreating with him. Marcus withdraws two steps, but doesn't look happy about it.

"We're just about to talk that over," Reid says. "If you'll excuse us."

"I'm part of this too," Marcus says, but his argument is as weak as his position and from the look on his face, he knows it.

"We'll let you know what we decide." Reid stands his ground. Leila joins him, Milo and Drew backing him up. The crowd of kids behind Marcus instantly retreats, accustomed to being told what to do, not making decisions of their own, leaving him alone. He snarls something under his breath full of so much bitterness Reid wonders about pushing him so hard. Still, Marcus follows the others and for now, that's all Reid cares about.

He watches him go, fading back into the tunnel, until he's no longer visible in the dark. Reid listens, to be sure no one is eavesdropping out there in the black, but is reasonably certain they are alone. Why it's so important he's not sure, except his level of trust is still bottomed out, especially where Marcus is concerned.

Reid turns back to the others.

"Plan?"

"Set a trap for the hunters and blow the crap out of them." Milo's voice is low and fierce, gritted teeth a flash in the low light, thin shoulders hunched forward as though that is the only thing keeping his built-up anxiety in.

"Agreed." Even Leila is turning savage on him. Reid has a moment of heat, rushing through him in a wave of attraction. She is so fiercely beautiful at that moment his heart wants him to kiss her.

Out of the question, of course it's out of the question. What is wrong with him? The moment passes because he makes it pass, and he is grateful the light is so dim because he is sure his face is flaming.

"Okay," Reid says, driving his mind back to the important matter of survival. "Good plan and I'm with you. There's nothing I want more than to have some payback. And blowing these bastards up would do the job nicely." Everyone grins at him. No, it isn't funny, not really. But he understands it. Is grinning himself, in fact. Can't help it. There is a certain joy in plotting the death of the hunters that shouldn't give him such satisfaction, but does.

Of course, dreaming about it and doing it are two different things. Reid hates to drag them down, but he needs them to think rationally. "Only one problem I can think of." He points down at the dynamite, all innocent there in the dirt, incognito to its ultimate purpose. "How do we light them?"

Milo's face falls while Leila lets out a little sigh of regret. But Drew snorts. "Got that covered. I have a lighter." He produces it from his front right pocket, the silver sides glinting in the light of the bulb between his filthy fingers.

Reid stares for a long time while Milo gapes and Leila's lips curve upward. Finally, Reid cuffs Drew on the back of the head very gently.

"Of course you do," he says.

"Sorry," Drew grins. "Didn't I mention that little tidbit before?"

23

They have a long and heated conversation by the light of that flickering bulb. Reid tries not to focus on the tight space, the stone and clay walls closing in around him, but on the argument at hand—how best to use the gift they've been given.

At first blowing up a few hunters is the consensus.

Until Drew points out one thing. "We still don't know if there's any bang in those things. What happens if we get a hunter in range and the damned stuff duds out?"

"Can't we test one?" Milo shivers, hopping up and down from one foot to the other, his eyes wandering over the ceiling. Reid realizes he isn't the only one who doesn't like it in the mine.

"And show our hand?" Drew shakes his head. He turns to look further into the tunnel. "We haven't explored this yet, either."

Reid is about to say a resounding no to that idea when Leila speaks up. "Why is there power in here? Doesn't that mean the hunters know about it?"

"For all we know it's their freaking home base." Milo's old attitude is returning, but Reid knows it's just stress and lets it go.

"Unlikely." Drew adjusts his glasses as he thinks. There are hollows in his cheeks where he was chubby before and his hands are lined, no longer plump. Reid takes a moment to admire his friend's courage and ability to keep up. And the brilliant mind behind the glasses. "I really think we should explore in here."

Reid agrees, but hates to admit it. "There's probably another way out," he says. "And might be a water source somewhere down here."

"But if the hunters catch us in here we're trapped." Milo shudders.

Leila slides one slim arm around the boy's shoulder and hugs him. "It's okay," she whispers. "Just think of it like a carnival funhouse."

"I hate the carnival," Milo says. "Too many damned clowns."

They all laugh, but Reid's dies early as he pictures the hunters in that role. He'll never think of clowns the same again.

"So maybe some of us explore while the rest look for the fence." Drew shakes his head before he's done speaking. "No that's stupid. We shouldn't split up." He sighs and looks at Reid. "What do you think?"

Just like that they are focused on him and he knows whatever he says they will do. Reid wants to run away, to find the fence and the gate and escape. But for some reason he can't bring himself to abandon this chance to maybe buy a little freedom and time to find another way out.

"Could this still be a working mine?" Reid asks. "From the other end I mean?"

Drew looks skeptical. "Doubt it."

Reid thinks about it another minute. "Okay, we have two choices, right? Go back out there and find the fence and maybe the gate. Or we try our luck in here and blow the entrance so the hunters can't get in."

They all look shocked. "Blow the entrance?" Milo's mouth hangs open. "Seal us in here?"

"The thing is," Reid says, "they may have set up the mine to trap us but they don't know we have a way to keep them out as much as us in." The more he thinks about it, the more he likes the idea. "Right? And mines, they have water sources, don't they? And there are always other exits. Always."

Drew is nodding even though he still looks like he wants to correct Reid's thinking. Leila just hugs Milo.

"Outside we're dead meat." Now that Joel's little pact is done the hunters will come after them just for spite. "In here, maybe we have a chance."

"To starve to death, or die in a cave-in," Milo says.

"True." Reid crosses his arms over his chest. "But those are our choices, so pick one."

No one says anything. Milo clears his throat after a moment while Drew shuffles his feet, small rocks making scratching noises on the stone floor of the tunnel. Leila finally sighs.

"We put it to a vote." Her eyes lift to Reid's. "We ask everyone what they want to do. This isn't a dictatorship. It's not even a democracy really." Her smile is small and wavering, but it's brave and Reid is grateful for it. "At this point it's all together or go it alone. Whatever we decide as a group, if someone disagrees, they can leave."

She is right, of course. They have no control over what the others want.

"All right, then," Reid says. "Let's go talk to them."

They emerge into full light and find the pack of kids huddled right at the mine mouth. Marcus sits a bit apart from them, shredding the bark from a stick. He meets Reid's eyes for only a second before dropping to focus back to what he is doing.

Reid lays out the plans to the group. When they hear about the fence, some are shocked but most, it turns out, know about it already.

"There's no gate," Marcus says.

"Actually, technically, there has to be." Drew goes into teacher mode. "Most likely more than one. Otherwise, how did they get us in here?"

No one argues.

Plan number two is greeted with far less enthusiasm. Some of the kids start to cry and Marcus actually leaps to his feet in protest.

"You're insane," he says, whole body trembling. "We won't have to wait on the hunters. You'll kill us all."

After that announcement, those who weren't crying start and those who were, sob. Reid wants to take the arrogant asshole and shake him. Instead he waits them out, long enough for their fear to cool down before going on.

"Those are our choices. It's that or sit here and wait for the hunters to get us. Because running is taking us nowhere. It's just wearing us down so we're easier to catch."

Someone hiccups past an indrawn breath, but no one challenges him. There's nothing to challenge. Reid is right and they all know it.

"The fence, then," Marcus says. "And your hypothetical gate."

Kids nod, wipe away tears and snot. Reid hears Drew sigh beside him and turns his head just a little, enough for the boy to whisper in his ear.

"They won't make it that far."

Drew is right, of course. Reid has no idea how long it's been since any of them had water. It's been over a day for him and he's feeling the effects again. The stream and the lake are both too far and too dangerous. Unless they can find another water source none of them will get to the fence, let alone be in any shape to make a plan to escape once they find the gate.

Reid decides to try one more time, using the last thread of hope he has been holding on to in an effort to convince them. "There's a chance," he doesn't want to lie to them, "that if we do find an exit from the mine, it will be on the other side of the fence."

He doesn't know it for sure. But he has a feeling this mine is their way out, a flaw in the hunter's plans. Especially if they can seal the entrance and keep the hunters out long enough to maneuver their way to the other side of the mountain.

He feels them sway toward him, but Marcus is quick to counter the change in mood.

"How do you know there's another way out?" He is through the pack, standing in front of Reid. Again the challenge hangs between them, Marcus too timid to grasp it physically, but having no problem using words.

"Of course there is," Drew answers for Reid. "There has to be. It's a safety thing. All mines have an extra exit."

Reid has almost won them thanks to Drew. He puts the final shove on the pack, speaking past Marcus. "You don't have to come. You can all decide and do what you want. But I'm going in the mine, with or without you. I'd rather face the uncertainty in there knowing at least I'm not being hunted than stay out here and run until I can't anymore. Until they catch me and gut me."

They don't get a chance to answer. The howl of a hunter does it for them.

The call is so close they panic and race into the mine as one. Reid shoves his way inside after them, calling for Drew. "The dynamite!" Drew is way ahead of him, letting the kids rush past, guarding the precious explosives with his body. Reid reaches him just as the last two kids run by and hears Drew grunt in pain. He clutches his left hand to his chest as Reid kneels beside him. One look tells Reid the bad news. Three fingers are bent at odd angles. He curses and tries to take Drew's hand, but the boy shakes his head, light flashing from his glasses.

"It's fine," he says. "Get the sticks."

Reid gathers them carefully and hurries back to the entrance, Drew on his heels. Marcus and a couple of the other kids are still there. He is speaking to Leila in a hushed whisper and she is listening. Nodding. Reid doesn't have time to think past the jab of jealousy that makes him flinch. She looks up when he emerges at a run before glancing away again. Is that guilt he saw on her face?

Milo tugs his arm. "They're coming!"

"Get inside," Reid says. "Watch the others. Make sure they don't go too far or get hurt." He spins back to Marcus as Milo takes a deep breath and plunges into the darkness.

“Still want to make a run for it?” A hunter howls. So close it makes Reid’s flesh crawl. But he holds his ground, six sticks of dynamite in his hands.

“I guess we’ll have to do it your way.” Marcus moves past Reid and disappears into the tunnel. Leila follows him. She hesitates next to Reid as though she is going to say something.

“We have to hurry.” He knows it comes out gruff, but he can’t deal with this right now. She bobs her head and leaves him there with Drew.

The boy still cradles his broken hand and looks as panicked as Reid feels.

“You’re not kidding.” His head comes up and he shudders when another howl echoes closer. The hunters have almost found them.

“What do I do?” Reid turns and looks at the mine entrance.

“We need to find holes to stick the dynamite in.” Drew points at one. “There, right there, see it?”

Reid does, though he is sure he wouldn’t have if Drew didn’t point it out. A small crack sits just past the entrance, only wide enough to shove the stick in sideways. The wick hangs out, dangling down.

"Great," Drew says, "now take the extra line and splice it on."

"What extra?" Reid spins on his friend and Drew groans.

"There was a spool of primer cord in that box," he says. "Here, leave these with me." Drew makes a pouch with the bottom of his t-shirt, using his healthy thumb and index finger on his left hand to do it. He hisses when Reid dumps in the weight of the five sticks. "Now go get it!"

Reid runs. He makes it to the rubble and the box in record time, barely registering that his breath is shallow, or the burn in his legs from the dash. He's just too used to being afraid for it to trouble him any more. He can hear the murmurs of the frightened kids and spots them just past the pile of dirt, waiting for him. But he can't think about them right now.

He hunts around for a bit, desperately looking for what Drew told him about and almost gives up before he spots the spool of thread-like cord lying on the other side of the tunnel. Someone must have kicked it during the dash for safety.

Reid grabs it and runs for the entrance, his heart lifting. Finally something is going right for a change.

24

When the tunnel entrance collapses in front of him, Reid is so shocked he almost doesn't stop himself in time. He has to back-pedal, crouch and cover to keep from being hurt or killed by the falling rubble. The entire front of the mine gives way with a horrible grinding and grumbling roll of destruction. It takes a moment for the rocks to settle, but Reid is already moving before they do—while calling out Drew's name.

He coughs and chokes on the dust, forcing his way forward, slamming his shins into sharp boulders, ankle aching from twisting over a clump of rocks. Reid's mind is empty of thoughts of himself, the pain a distant cry he ignores. He can only think of the boy he left behind at the tunnel mouth, his friend now somewhere in the wreckage.

Reid forces his way on, the spool of cord still clutched in his hand. It's almost completely dark in the tunnel now, most of the entry blocked by chunks of rock and debris, only thin lines of light seeping through the cracks, dust swirling in the penetrating shafts of sun.

"Drew!" Reid spits out a wad of dirt, lungs burning for another reason. "Drew!"

"H-here."

Reid spots a familiar penny loafer and dives for it. He travels up the boy's leg to his chest and finally finds his head. There is enough light to see him by, a convenient beam reaching the rocks above his face as Reid forces a large stone out of his path so he can reach his friend.

Reid gasps at the sight of Drew and draws back, heart clenching, mind fleeing from the truth.

Drew's mouth is coated in blood, his glasses askew, one lens shattered. And still he manages a lopsided smile even as he struggles for air. "Hey, Reid."

"Drew." Reid leans closer, forces himself to look at the full extent of the damage. A large rock rests on the boy's chest, several others pinning his legs. Reid's first impulse is to shift the main one, but Drew cries out so horribly when he tries, Reid stops.

"I can't… I can't feel my legs." Drew's breath comes out in

short, heavy pants, the pain each one causes him written all over his face. "I think my back is broken."

Drew swims in Reid's vision as tears well and pour down his cheeks, dripping onto his friend's chest. Reid reaches out, one hand gentle on Drew's shoulder. Instantly, as though that light pressure released a dam, a pool of blood gathers around the edges of the rock, spreading over Drew's T-shirt. Reid pulls his hand back, but whether he caused it or it was simply inevitable, what's done is done.

"I'm sorry, I'm so sorry." Reid rocks back and forth a moment. "Drew, please, you have to be okay."

Drew tries to answer him, but his mouth is full of blood, it's running down his chin and over his neck, pooling in his collarbone. Reid can't stand it, reaches for the rock again, attempts to pull the stone free. Someone's hands are on him, tugging him backward. He fights against those hands until he realizes they are Leila's.

"We have to help him." Reid can't stop crying. She is crying too, and Milo just behind her. The rest of the kids pile up in the dark, watching, silent. Marcus doesn't say a word, just stares at Drew with a blank expression.

Leila crouches next to the dying boy. "Oh, Drew," she whispers.

Reid pulls her back away from their friend so hard she stumbles and Marcus has to catch her.

"We have to get him out!" Reid's shout brings a shower of fresh rocks and dirt down on them, but he doesn't care. Some of the kids flee back inside the tunnel, but most remain, eyes locked on the bleeding kid under the rubble. Reid swings back to Drew. "We'll get you out, okay? Don't worry."

Drew coughs and blood spews over the stones, bright red droplets shining in the shaft of sunlight for an instant before they fall. "Reid." His voice is barely a whisper. "Reid."

Reid sobs once and falls down next to Drew, clutching at his right hand. He feels it then, the hard smooth shape of the lighter. Drew's eyes meet his. Close. Open slowly.

"One of the sticks… was damaged… didn't notice… too late…"

Reid just holds his hand.

"You have to go." Drew coughs again, weaker this time. His breathing is harsh, bubbly. The pool on his chest has soaked his shirt and now joins the blood from his mouth, running from his collarbone over his shoulder into the darkness and dust.

"No." Reid shakes his head so hard he feels pain shoot

through his temples. No. He can't. Not Drew. Not now. He will not leave his friend behind.

Reid won't survive another loss. He's sure of it.

Drew pulls his hand free and flicks open the top of the lighter. That's when Reid notices the dynamite sticking out of the rubble next to him. "I can… make sure… they don't… follow you."

Reid tries to take the lighter away, but Drew is oddly fast for someone so close to death. "I don't… want them to… eat me." It's a whisper. As if he doesn't want anyone else to hear. "Please, Reid. I can't let them… do that. Okay? Please?"

That's it then, and Reid knows it. There is so much blood and Drew's pale light is fading fast. Reid steps back, allows Milo a moment. They whisper together, quickly, solemnly, before Milo retreats back down the tunnel. Leila is next and Reid may not be able to hear her words, but he can't miss the sound of her grief. It colors her last soft moment with their friend before she too leaves, Marcus trailing along behind her.

Reid stays. Holds Drew's hand. Can't let go.

"You have to," Drew says. "It's time, Reid." The howl of a hunter punctuates his point. It sounds like they are just outside the hole. Something snuffles on the other side of the light. And yet Reid hangs on and hangs on, unable to leave Drew behind.

"If you don't... leave... I'm taking you... with me." Drew strikes the lighter once, twice. It takes him three tries to get it lit and Reid understands. It is time.

"I forgive you." It's terribly important Drew knows. "For the cave. For not trusting me."

Drew's last smile brings Reid's tears back. "Thanks. Me too. Now run, you idiot."

Drew's shaking hand descends, the flame touching the wick. Stones rattle, the light gets brighter, sun shining full in Reid's face. He feels a shadow fall over him and glances out the small, fresh opening, widened from the one left behind by the explosion.

A hunter grins back.

Reid runs, heart breaking for leaving his friend despite the boy's forgiveness, hears Drew manage a thin shout that reaches him just before the shock-wave does.

"Eat this, you bastards!"

The blast picks Reid up and sends him forward, the bright flash searing his peripheral vision just before he squeezes his eyes shut. Reid throws his arms up as he is propelled into the pile of debris face-first, the splintered wood from the dynamite box digging into his stomach. Reid huddles small, covers his head with his arms, shielding himself from the heat and raining debris. The whole place shudders for a long time before falling still.

It takes him a while to drag himself to his feet. He'd rather lie there forever and not go on. But he does it for Drew, because his friend would want him to, because he would have done the same for Reid. He retraces his steps to the end of the tunnel and stands there for a bit, examining the now-plugged entry for signs of light.

Nothing. Drew did it. He saved them. Reid bows his head and hugs himself, fresh tears tracking through the dirt on his face.

"You did good," Reid whispers, just like his father used to say to him. "Nice job, kiddo." He lets out a deep sigh, letting his grief nestle in his heart where he will hold the memory of Drew forever.

When he is finally ready, Reid turns and follows the tunnel to join the others.

Visit Patti Larsen for more new releases

Connect online at

http://www.pattilarsen.com

http://www.pattilarsenbooks.blogspot.com

Check out this sample of the exciting sequel

Excerpt Copyright © 2011 by Patti Larsen

1

The last of the dust has settled. Reid coughs what is left of it from his lungs and huddles by himself in the flickering light of the weak bulb. The tunnel walls are rough and far from comfortable to lean against but he has nothing else so he lives with it.

Most of the kids have stopped crying at least. Since the blast closed the entrance, they've shivered together in terror that the ceiling will fall in on them. Reid doesn't care about it, not any more. He thinks he would happily die now if it meant he didn't have to live with Drew's sacrifice.

When they first met, Reid never would have thought the short, pudgy kid with the glasses and braces and ridiculous penny-loafers would make it even a minute out there in the forest. But Drew's tenacity surprised Reid at every turn, and his brains and logical thinking kept Reid moving in the right direction. Reid never intended to let the kid get to him, to pierce his need to guard his heart against loss. The deaths of the first kids he met in this insane game of cat and mouse made him hesitate to even travel with anyone else. But something about Drew's steady good nature despite everything he went through was enough to dull Reid's defenses and let the brilliant and funny kid in.

Which makes it all the worse, of course. Drew was brilliant. Smarter than any of them. Knew all about explosives and the military and alien invasions, even if the latter made his friends roll their eyes at him.

They need Drew, now more than ever. Need his insight, his head for details. Without him, Reid feels like he's on his own again, no matter that a crowd of kids waits for him to pull himself together.

It should have been Reid that died. There's no way around that truth. And it's all his fault. Drew found the old mine but it was Reid's idea to hide in there, to close off the exit rather than seeking out the fence as had been his plan all along. The huge, hot fence Reid is still sure has a gate they might use to escape the giant forest hunting ground. But he had to convince Drew this was a good idea. And if he had just protected his friend from the stampede of kids when the hunters showed up at the mouth of the mine, the boy's hand wouldn't have been broken. And it would have been Reid placing the unstable and ancient dynamite, not Drew with his crippled fingers.

It would have been Reid who was crushed by a pile of rock after a defective stick went off on its own. Not Drew.

Reid squeezes his eyes shut and turns his head from the light, longing for the darkness to swallow him up. But he can't escape the glow. It hovers there in the periphery of his vision, taunting him like a ghost of the outdoors.

This is his fault, too. Them being trapped. It was his bright idea to blow the cave entrance, to lock them inside and the hunters out. But now here they are, alone in the darkness, with no idea if there is even a way to escape. Reid isn't fooling himself. Yes, there may be another exit. That idea is a good one. But this mine looks really old and for all he knows the secondary entrance is collapsed as well.

Reid doesn't want to think about any of that, though. Drew is dead. His friend is gone. His heart can't take any more.

Reid lets his eyes drift open. Not like it's doing him any good anyway. He sees Leila in the low light, drifting from kid to kid, talking to them, offering what comfort she can. He remembers the first time he met her, in a cave ironically. So pale she glowed. She still glows, her thin blonde hair and white, white skin shining in the dim light. She glances his way but he won't keep her gaze, he can't. That memory of their introduction is full of Drew. Besides, he's too afraid she blames him as much as he does himself.

As his eyes leave her, they fall on Marcus. Reid's not the only one watching Leila. The Hispanic guy's attention never leaves her. Jealousy surges in Reid's stomach, punching through to his chest. And more than that. Distrust. Marcus was part of the problem that put them here in the first place. He stood second to Joel, the bully who sacrificed kids to the hunters to save his own ass. And Marcus challenges Reid every chance he gets. Now he has his dirty eyes on Leila. The surge of emotion, layered over Reid's grief, is too much to bear.

Instead of overreacting and attacking Marcus, Reid is only able to huddle tighter into himself and let it seethe inside him. He finds himself wondering all over again what the hell he is doing there. What any of them are doing there. Dumped in the wilderness, hunted and killed by men who aren't men at all but some kind of intelligent animals that only look human. And for the first time in a long time, Reid thinks about his sister Lucy. It's her fault he's here, his mind tries to tell him, his blame bouncing to a new target. But he's never been able to hold anger against her. And if her new boss, Mr. Syracuse, did sell them out to whoever is running this horrible experiment, she's as much a victim as Reid.

Fresh out of foster care, he should have known better than to trust the set up Lucy found herself in. No way could someone like her land a job with benefits like a new convertible and a swank apartment downtown. No way.

And so, yet again, the blame ricochets back, landing with a thud of reality on Reid. Stupid. Stupid and naïve.

When Marcus gets to his feet, Reid barely notices, he is so wrapped up in his personal torment.

"All right," Marcus says, voice low but arrogance clearly showing through. "Everyone up. We're moving on."

Some of the kids groan, but most of them obey slowly, moving like little old people rather than the teenagers they are. Reid doesn't even think about paying attention to what Marcus wants. He certainly doesn't recognize the other guy as any kind of authority over him. But he can't muster the energy to stand up to Marcus so he keeps his peace. Even when Milo tries to get his attention, skinny Milo with his jet-black skin and giant eyes, Reid refuses to budge. He's counting on Marcus making an ass of himself anyway and is looking forward to it.

At this point he'll take all the entertainment he can get.

Milo sighs, looking disappointed, and turns away to join the others. Only Leila holds back.

"We need to talk first." Reid isn't sure why he's surprised she is the one to speak up but he is.

"About what?" Marcus doesn't sound like he's in the mood to talk but Leila doesn't back down. Reid wants to laugh at the look on the guy's face but it would take too much effort so he just watches.

"What our plans are." She glances at Reid briefly but doesn't leave her eyes on him for long.

"Thanks to someone we know, we don't have much of a choice of plans." Marcus isn't being very subtle in his faintly British accented voice. Reid couldn't care less.

"I disagree." Leila's calm is infectious. Reid finds himself paying attention to her, his emotions easing somewhat.

"Fine, princess," Marcus says. "You tell us your amazing ideas."

Reid is on his feet, his anger finally winning. He slams Marcus into the wall of the tunnel right next to the wavering bulb of light, face so close he can see the dirt ground into the other guy's pores.

"Shut the hell up," Reid says so softly only Marcus can hear him, "and show some respect."

That sullen expression Reid is used to falls over Marcus's face. Like he wants to strike out but doesn't have the guts.

"What's the matter," Reid says, louder this time, on purpose. "Scared of me or something?"

Marcus is shaking. Reid holds him up against the wall another moment before letting him go and stepping away. He turns to Leila and nods once. But the look on her face makes him wonder if he should have acted at all. She is so disgusted she spins away from him, crossing her arms over her chest.

Milo, meanwhile, is grinning, white teeth flashing in the light. He gives Reid a thumbs up.

"If you two are done being jerks," she says, "we have more important things to talk about."

Reid backs off again, knowing she's right.

"Go ahead," he says.

She relents, turning back toward him, her expression softer. "We're all sad about Drew." Reid doesn't move or say anything while the rest of the kids mutter stuff that doesn't matter. He wants to tell them to shut up, the whole lot of them. Like they gave a crap about his friend. Only Milo and Leila matter there. Marcus stays quiet and Reid is grateful. Had the other guy tried to say anything about Drew Reid would have had to kill him and he knows Leila wouldn't like that.

"But we need to go back to the entrance and make sure it's sealed before we do anything." Reid doesn't bother telling her he's done so already. "Once we're sure the hunters can't get in, then we go forward."

Marcus's sullen expression softens. "You're right," he says. Not like it makes Reid trust him or anything but at least he's stopped being a jerk to Leila.

"Then what?" Milo is looking right at Reid. "What do we do?"

He decides in that moment he's done. Reid has no desire to be responsible for any of them ever again. There is no way he's getting another kid killed. Reid looks away from Milo's expectation and finds the rest of the kids looking at him the same way.

Marcus is scowling so deeply his face might implode. Reid would pay a lot of money to see that happen. If he had any. But that incentive isn't enough. Not nearly enough.

"Why don't you ask Marcus?" Reid shrugs his shoulders and turns away. "He seems to want to play follow the leader."

Their disappointment hits Reid like a physical blow, all that emotion washing over him as they sigh, hesitate and turn away.

"That's right," Marcus snaps. "Look where he's gotten us so far. And you want him to tell you what to do?" The shift is slow but it happens and Reid regrets it even while he accepts it as necessary for his own survival. "Now, listen up. I'm going to send some of you to check out the blast site. The rest of us will stay here and wait for your report." Reid rolls his eyes. Of course Marcus has no intention of going himself.

Coward.

"Maybe we should all go," Leila says but Marcus cuts her off.

"No, too dangerous." He fixes his dark eyes on Reid. "You'll take these three," he points out a few kids at random, "and have a look."

Reid ignores him while the two boys and scrawny girl complain softly.

"Shut up," Marcus snaps. "You heard me. Now follow orders. You!" Reid fakes a yawn and sighs, still ignoring the obvious. Marcus covers the distance between them in three steps but doesn't get in Reid's face. It's like he knows he can't win but feels the need to bully.

Reid meets his eyes in a lazy lift of his own. "Don't tell me what to do. Ever."

Marcus's jaw works and Reid can hear his teeth grinding together. He looks like he wants to say something but finally spins away and focuses on Milo.

"Fine, you go. And hurry up. We need to get moving."

Milo reluctantly follows orders, drifting past Reid with a scowl on his face.

"Can I suggest something?" The kids all look the same to Reid but he tries to put a name to this one. He finally does just as Marcus nods like he's God or something.

Cole.

"So, I was thinking about the electricity." The boy speaks very fast, his dirty-blonde hair falling forward into his eyes as he talks, forcing him to toss his head like an unhappy pony. "If we can find where it's coming from, maybe it will lead us to a way out."

Smart thinking. From the sighs and smiles around him, the other kids are relieved to have such a concrete goal.

Reid doesn't want to get sucked into their plans but this kid stands out. He immediately smothers his ability to care about anyone new. No way is he going there again.

Marcus must have sensed the shift away from him and does his best to ruin it. "Of course," he says like the kid is stupid or something. "Kind of obvious."

Hope dies along with free will. Everyone else shuffles their feet and acts like they aren't there. This must be how Joel controlled them. Bullying and belittling. Reid's dislike of the Hispanic guy climbs another mountain. He's as much a waste of humanity as Joel was.

Reid meets Leila's eyes. She is troubled, he can tell, but she looks away as quickly as he does and he chalks it up to her hating him.

Has to be that. He hates himself so why would she feel any different?

It's not long before Milo and his three trailing companions return.

"There's no way out." Milo says like it's a death sentence. As far as they all know it could be. Everyone falls so silent Reid can hear the buzzing of the light bulb as it flickers its life away.

"You heard him," Marcus says. "Time to move on. You,"

he points at Cole and the boy perks, "keep an eye on that line." He jerks his thumb at the electric cable. Like it's going anywhere. Again laughter bubbles up in Reid's chest but he manages to hold it back.

Somehow he doesn't think Marcus would appreciate it. And not that Reid really cares but he's too tired and wrung out to do anything about it if the other guy finally decides to challenge him.

When Marcus leads off, the troop of tired and filthy kids trails after him. Leila glances over her shoulder at Reid from where she walks beside Marcus. Milo refuses to meet his eyes at all.

Reid watches them go and waits until they are almost out of sight before he follows.

Made in the USA
Charleston, SC
16 October 2012